I0729795

MACON'S LAKE

MACON'S LAKE

ADLYNN ASTER

Macon's Lake (1st ed.)
By Adlynn Aster
Edited by Annie M. Huber
Cover illustration & design by Adlynn Aster
ISBN-13: 979-8-9943634-2-3
Copyright Adlynn Aster 2025
LCCN: Pending
© 2025 Adlynn Aster. All Rights Reserved.
No part of this publication may be reproduced, stored in a retrieval system, or transmitted in any form or by any means without prior written permission from the author.
For permission requests or to reach the author's team, email heythere@adlynnaster.com.
Disclaimer: This is a work of fiction. Any resemblance to actual persons, living or dead, is purely coincidental. Sort of.

DEDICATION

For those who've been left behind to bear the memories.

Other Books by Adlynn Aster

The Boss Goddess series:

Boss Moves
Boss Witch
Boss Battle
Magritte's Gift

Visit AdlynnAster.com for more information.

1

Fellchaser

(n.) A long-forgotten mistake from your past that could reappear at any time and rip your life apart, like a boomerang you tossed away years ago that's only just now looping back around, which you'd have no idea how to handle because you have no idea what it is.

The iPhone buzzed in the darkness. Its screen threw a blue glow across the wall as it worked its way toward the edge of the nightstand in slow semi-circles. Two mounds of sleeping human bodies stirred in unison as the device continued to hum against the table.

George reached out and snagged it just before it buzzed itself off into the small wicker trash can below. She propped herself up on one arm. A lock of pale hair fell over her eyes and she brushed it back, squinting at the bright screen. She frowned at the unfamiliar number and clocked the time: 2:47AM. 317 – Indiana area code. *Hm.* Whatever it was, it wasn't good, if someone from Indy was calling at this hour.

She answered, her voice thick with sleep. "Hello?" There was a brief pause on the other end of the line and then, a ragged breath.

"Well, you better come get these kids, Georgia Lane." George immediately became more alert, her heartbeat ratcheted up a notch. "Hannah's dead," said the low, gravelly voice, a woman – George finally registered who it was and sat up straighter, clasping the phone against her face.

"Aunt Carla?" George exhaled.

"ODed in a fuckin' Burger King bathroom," Aunt Carla continued. "Fentanyl. Ain't like we didn't see it comin', but dammit..." She paused. "Them boys ain't goin' into the foster system. On my dyin' breath, Georgie."

George opened her mouth but couldn't summon a sound. On the other end of the line, she heard a noisy intake of breath and the crackle of Aunt Carla's long cigarette as she took it down half an inch. George closed her eyes. Next to her, the body beneath the thick comforter began to snore softly. Carla took her silence as an invitation to continue.

"I'm all ate up with this cancer, m'self or I'd keep 'em – you know that," she said, matter-of-factly. "Finally stopped with the chemo, couple-few weeks back, cause it ain't doin' shit 'cept makin' me *feel* like shit. You know." She took another deep drag. Exhaled. "Ain't nobody left but you, Georgie."

"I'll... I'll figure it out," George whispered, gathering herself. "I'll be there."

"I know." Aunt Carla's voice softened, "I know you will, punkin'." She paused for a long moment, and George imagined her extinguishing the smoldering butt against the inside of the large, yellow glass ashtray that had sat in the middle of the battered wood kitchen table since it still lived at Grandma's.

"You'll stay with me when you come. I'll keep the boys 'til then."

Georgia's mouth worked silently. "Okay," she managed.

"See you soon, Georgie." Carla hung up with a soft click. George realized her aunt must still be on a landline and wondered at that for several seconds before her stomach clenched.

She rolled off the bed, landed hard on all fours, and retched into the trash can.

Of all the fucking weeks she was needed on-site for studio sessions, after four months of spoiling away at home, it had to be this one. George tried to focus. She stood at the wall of glass overlooking Sunset, that western stretch in the brief and disconcerting hinterlands between all the posh shops and cafes, but before the jewel-green lawns and mansions of Beverly Hills. The tiny cars below inched forward bit by bit as the sun angled along its length, toward the horizon, slanting gold down the long four-lane road. The start of evening rush hour. Her golden-brown eyes were unfocused as she looked down, her mind elsewhere. Behind her was a long, polished wood conference table surrounded by sleek, comfortable chairs. She slid her fashionably large, thick-rimmed, red glasses down and rubbed the bridge of her nose. Weariness smudged the skin beneath her lower lashes so darkly that even her foundation couldn't mask it. She made a tactical decision that morning to forgo eyeliner and mascara out of caution, opting for a French red power lip that matched her glasses and the bottoms of her understated, expensive heels.

But she hadn't cried yet. She felt nothing at all, not after the initial sense of dread and realization of what was happening finally washed over her. For all the preparation and discussion around the potential of this happening, the situation seemed incomprehensible now. George hadn't spoken to Hannah in over a month, and had never suspected, given that Hannah was so far along in the pregnancy with her third child, that she was still using. She shook her head slightly as a flash of anger ran through her body. *Blame.* She desperately needed someone to blame. She needed to burn things down and wrest some kind of justice from this situation.

Instead, George stood silent and motionless, her body taut, and regarded the traffic below with a detached gaze as she blazed within. She didn't have to worry about rush hour anymore, because she was in before it started and out long after it ended, which was saying something, being in LA. She remembered what it was like before all this. She traded in traffic, band practice, late shows, a wide circle of friends, spontaneous drinks, and weekends, all for her current enviable position with Weber Records. She never looked back, never considered what may have been lost. She made an intentional practice of not considering it.

Hundreds of people probably would literally kill to get her job; the pay, the notoriety, the perks. But it was she who landed it, and held on to it, made it hers, made her name, fighting for every molecule of respect she accumulated. There was no fucking way anyone would find weakness in her now – she'd worked too hard. It was her ability to turn off her emotions that had gotten her through the hardest times in her life, up to this moment, which was supremely fucked.

Death happens, she thought. *There's no reason to stop the world.* George spotted her boss and mentor, Lucia, striding gracefully down the hallway, toward George's office. Lucia was everything Georgia aspired to. Career success. A fierce negotiator and exemplary leader. Confident bearing, an uncanny ability to craft a perfect response to anything on the spot. Lucia's manner, and the effortless way these qualities all seemed to come together, appeared as instinctual as breathing. Even her aesthetic was flawless. Cream, wide-leg pants hugged slender hips, a beautifully woven sweater hung from her tall, willowy frame, her silver hair was tousled in a perfectly messy shag. Large, black-framed eyeglasses lent the whole look a feeling of edginess. At fifty-six, Lucia, who was already a stunner in her youth, was in the prime of her life. George had never known anyone who wielded power and influence so deftly. George bit her lip, her brows gathering in the center, and cocked her hip out, turning back to the glass to study her own hourglass shape. She frowned at her reflection, which exaggerated everything, as the door swung open. A cool rush of air swept through the room.

"Do these pants make my ass look big… bigger? Do they hang right at the waistline?" George continued to frown at the faint reflection of herself, as a heavy, buzzing numbness settled over her body. Dry wool filled her brain.

"The waist is snatched and your ass looks fat and delicious. I'd eat it," Lucia stated. "Now, tell me what's happened, dear."

"I just inherited two children, and I have to go to Indiana to fetch them," George said glibly.

Lucia inhaled sharply. "What in god's name are you talking about?"

"My cousin died." She felt the flatness in her expression and struggled to hold onto it. A flash of a memory: Hannah when she was eight, white-blonde ponytail swinging in the sunshine, clutching a baby bunny to her chest and running full bore toward the muddy creek at the tree line. The one near the bottom of pastures filled with Queen Ann's Lace and tall daisies. Her heart skipped a beat and ached unbearably for a second before she recovered.

Lucia studied her face. "I fail to understand why that statement is followed by 'and now her children belong to me'?"

George looked at her, and raised her hands to her waist, palms out, pleading, then let them fall. She shook her head and struggled to catch her breath, reaching out to the metal window beam to steady herself.

"There's no one else…"

"Oh, George, you don't have to—"

"I'm their legal guardian," she heard herself saying. "I signed papers." Lucia stood in expectant silence while George listened to her heart pounding in her ears. "Five years ago, right after her second was born. She had a seizure at the grocery store – turned out she was still using. She had… other problems. That was right about when Aunt Carla started chemo for the first time. Then Uncle Steven died, my dad died by suicide a decade ago, and my grandparents were just too old. We thought it would be wise to take precautions… considering what happened with my cousin Henry's kids, and I…" George felt dizzy and stopped, reaching out to steady herself with one hand on the conference table. "I signed the papers."

"What about your aunt – isn't she already taking care of them?"

"Cancer," Georgia said grimly, her mouth setting in a thin line. "She doesn't have much longer. Everyone else is dead."

A lock of her thick, ash blonde hair escaped her bun, and she used the next several seconds to fix it while she bought some time to formulate her thoughts. The string of tragedies her family had endured rarely surfaced in a way that caused her pain, but it pushed up now, straining against her diaphragm and tightening her stomach muscles. She willed it to subside.

"You can't…" Lucia paused, considering her words carefully. "You can't just take on two traumatized kids…" She gestured helplessly. "I mean, come on, George, what would your life even look like? How would that work?" She moved across the room and laid a slender, manicured hand on George's shoulder. George squeezed her eyes shut and tried to control her breathing. She hated being touched when she was hurting; it made controlling her reactions so much more difficult.

"I'll make it work. There's no choice."

Lucia made a sympathetic noise in her throat.

"I love kids," George added, after just a long enough pause that it landed awkwardly. "It's not like I can't do it. I'd be good at it." For some reason, saying it aloud made her blush defensively.

"What's Kato have to say about this?"

George thought back to that morning, when she shook her fiancé awake. He placed a warm hand on her back and uttered understanding things, echoing her words: *We'll figure it out.* Kato was nothing, if not accommodating.

She needed to get a grip before this crushed her. She found herself, too often these days – even before now – ducking into dark corners and bathroom stalls, any hidden nook where she could catch her breath. Hiding to stave off encroaching panic attacks, out of sight of anyone who might smell blood in the water. Away from those who would make sympathetic noises or view her with pity. She didn't know what was breaking her; maybe it was just the world.

Kato caught her sitting in her home office, shoulders shaking silently, on more than one occasion recently. Packed as they were into the space of their small condo, which was never meant to serve as 24-7 living and workspace for two grown humans and a cat, it would have been impossible for him not to, no matter how hard she tried to hide her stress.

Kato had been at her side for ten years, with too many shared adventures, victories, and tragedies to keep track of anymore. He knew she didn't like to talk about her feelings. Not the big ones, at least.

Tactful partner that he was, he avoided open acknowledgment of her quiet suffering. He simply made cups of hot tea appear wordlessly before her, or left nourishing snacks while she worked, touched her in gentle, safe ways that wouldn't cause unwanted emotions to well up, taking his cues from her expressions and moods. His tender and unobtrusive attention kept her going. He was good like that. An unexpected lump rose in her throat.

"George?"

"Sorry. We discussed this – before I agreed. This isn't ideal, but it's not totally unexpected."

"Honey."

George turned and regarded Lucia. "It's fine. I'm fine." She looked up and tried a small smile. "Really. It's just – it might take some time to get things worked out. They'll be with their grandma – my Aunt Carla – until I handle the legal stuff." She searched Lucia's face for a reaction. "But I'm not sure I can be here for the Jung Karl launch."

Lucia moved to a nearby chair and settled into it like a butterfly, flicking her wrist dismissively. "That's the last thing you need to worry about right now." She threw George a shrewd look as she fingered the hem of her sweater. "No one will even notice you're not there, darling, and I mean that in the kindest way possible. You don't need to prove yourself to anyone. You're in a position now that is… virtually unassailable." She met George's eyes. "Take as long as you need."

"Thank you," George murmured. Lucia, thirteen years her senior, knew better than most how hard it was to carve out a place for herself in an industry that remained firmly male-dominated. She'd always strived to please her, and Lucia was never disappointed. The pair's friendship was iconic, but George's fight to secure her own place was far from over. At the end of the day, she was Lucia's protégé, and Lucia was still her boss. *Indebted* was an appropriate descriptor for her relationship to the older woman.

Lucia suddenly perked up in her chair. "George. I just had a thought – and you can tell me if it's not appropriate."

George, who already knew she'd do whatever was about to be requested, raised one eyebrow.

"You know Ben Macon?"

"I know who he is," she said evasively. She turned back to the window and watched the line of cars creep along the roadway below.

"He's one of Marshall's artists. He's up in Michigan right now – we put him up in a vacation rental to work on his album and he's a month overdue. We already have creative out for a late November digital release. What do you think about heading up there while you're in the region? See if you can light a fire under his ass. Is that… asking too much? He's been impossible to communicate with, and he needs a strong hand. This will be his last album with us, so we're eager to wrap it up."

She inwardly groaned. Macon wasn't a good guy, and she wasn't a fan. But George knew she'd be glad for something work-related that might keep her distracted here and there, so she was sure she could manage to put on her big girl pants and handle the man. It should be easy to whip him into shape, given how little she gave a fuck about what he thought of her.

She flashed a tight smile at Lucia. "Of course. No problem. I have the horn and strings sessions tomorrow, so I'll leave after that. I should probably figure out my plane tickets and – everything else. Get me Macon's info and I'll head up there next Monday."

"Put everything on the company card. Have Blake arrange all the travel." Lucia rose and moved toward the door. She paused at the threshold. "Call if you need anything, dear."

George leaned her forehead against the glass and closed her eyes.

Hiraeth

(n.) A deep sense of longing for a home or homeland that
is lost and cannot be returned to, or perhaps a longing for
a time, place, or person that is beyond reach.

George sped down the rural road. There were still places
like this in the middle of the country, but markedly
fewer now than when she was a kid. She nursed a melan-
cholic mood as she made her way through the city from the
airport. She drove past where Rosalyn's Bakery used to be,
where grandma used to take her for the chocolate eclairs;
and Swanson's Grocery, that grandma swore had the only
chicken quarters in town worth buying; and Sutton's, with
their huge, rich eggs for eight cents each, even in 2018. That
was the last time she'd visited before Grandma was gone.
After that, she hadn't been able to bear coming back. But
she suspected the eggs stayed the same price until Sutton's
closed its doors.

The old family farm store now housed an H&R Block.
Its soft, green lightbox logo hovered above, looking incon-
gruously modern at the edge of a soybean field that would
probably give way to neat rows and cul-de-sacs of identical
tract homes within the year.

Those other hallowed childhood favorites were now
five generations of failed strip malls past; the bakery first
becoming a Blockbuster, then some other things, then a

GameStop, and now, a QDoba, whatever the fuck that was. The others went the same way as the local Walmart slowly leached the life out of the surrounding communities. The family-owned businesses eventually shuttered, to be replaced with an endless rise and fall of homogeneous chains and franchises.

But there were a few stretches to be found that the developers hadn't yet claimed. Country roads where you could drive for miles and pass just a few old farmhouses set off neat, emerald lawns bordered by hollyhock and bridal bush. Where rows of corn extended past them; rows so long the far edge of the fields disappeared into the low mist that hung over the corn silk in the mornings and at dusk. Or backed by thick bands of trees – the remaining survivors of the old temperate forests, now barely kissed by autumn's first chill.

She rolled the windows down and unbound her hair. It was a pretty day, 80 degrees, balmy, the blue sky shot with little, puffy clouds. It slammed her back to her eighteenth summer, which she remembered with the clarity of a silver bell. It was her last summer unmarked by crushing sorrow. She remembered holding the wheel loosely, smoking cigarettes and driving these same roads. She still knew the wide curve that was coming and how fast she could speed into it and take it safely.

The ghosts of her younger cousins, the last of them now only three days dead, laughed in the passenger and back seats. They laughed as George sped smoothly through the bends where moonlight filtered through the trees to land like glitter on the pavement. They laughed while they drank warm beer in the dark baseball field, that they stole from Grandpa's garage fridge. They laughed at her city-girl sympathy for the dead racoon on the side of the road, they laughed as they fumbled the dial around for a radio station with any good music at that hour. They laughed because it was summer, and because they were all together again for her yearly pilgrimage to Indy. They laughed because they were kids, and they hadn't yet learned how hard the world would treat them.

Warm air streamed through her hair, and she was buried in a bittersweet wash of nostalgia. George's mind opened up as she flew down the road. Concerns she refused to confront back home pushed to the forefront of her thoughts.

Her life felt like a tangled fucking mess, all raw emotion roiling under the surface of a neatly managed facade. She'd watched helplessly as friends around her fell to pieces during the pandemic. She ministered to the needs of her chosen family as best she could, even while her work threatened to consume her. When it did, she continued to exist for everyone but herself.

And still, figuratively killing herself to be available didn't stop her people from literally killing themselves. Others terminally succumbed in other ways. She'd sure as shit seen the full range in the past year. Cancer, suicides, overdoses, the virus, cardiac failure, an auto accident, a fatal event involving inebriation and a staircase, and all the various ways of killing oneself and dying that fell in between. Her closest inner circle and family dwindled alarmingly. She felt desperately alone, but somehow less alone than she craved.

Somewhere in her heart, George recognized that, despite her misgivings on timing, being away from home and work responsibilities would be good for her. As long as Ben Macon wasn't too much of a pain in the ass. It would give her a needed breath to ground herself before this ensuing shit storm. She tried to lean into it, not to yearn for the distraction of a phone call and someone else's urgent need. It was hard to break the dynamic of needing to be needed, though, and she struggled.

All the same, she relished the spaciousness she had to confront her thoughts as she drove. It struck her that when she stopped commuting, she no longer had hours of dead time to process her thoughts at the beginning and end of each workday. Most days, she rolled out of bed and into routine at 5am, leaping from one task to the next. Make coffee, workout, shower, daily virtual briefing, endless emails, a punishing barrage of virtual meetings and calls. In the mornings she briefed with Lucia for the day as she applied her makeup. Minutes that were completely her own were so rare she forgot how good it felt.

George slowed and turned off onto a long, gravel drive bracketed at the entrance by old weeping willows. Their long tendrils were just beginning to yellow as summer faded. As she neared the house, the front screen swung open and revealed a tiny, shriveled form in a pink, quilted house dress. The ever-present cigarette curled smoke up from a pinkly lacquered set of claws as Aunt Carla waved with her free hand.

Sandy, Aunt Carla's yappy dog, pushed the screen door open and tore out full bore, howling fiercely at George's driveway intrusion. George watched the screen door.

"Michael and Jack," she muttered to herself, pulling the boys' names to the front of her memory. She parked and the car's engine slowly cooled, a series of clicks into silence as she stared through the windshield at the stranger before her, looking back and forth between her aunt and the house. She waited to catch a glimpse of Hannah's sons behind the screen. No – my sons, she thought, with a sudden wave of terror.

The next thing she knew, Aunt Carla was in her window, smiling, her eyes wet, grasping at the door handle, opening it. Extracting her and enfolding her into an impossibly strong hug with her impossibly thin, wasted arms. George took a deep breath of her rosewater / cigarette / Tide detergent scent and melted into the hug as Aunt Carla murmured against her hair.

"Oh, my sweet girl. My sweet girl. I'm so happy to see you." Her voice, thick in the back of her throat with grief, sickness, and Illinois accent, cracked. "I sure wish things was different. Oh, my girl."

3

Yeorie

(n.) A certain scent that has the power to sweep you back
to childhood.

George awoke to sunlight streaming through patchwork
quilt curtains. The voices of small humans, and the
pounding of their feet as they ran across the worn wood
floors, floated up to her in the attic bedroom. She sat up in
bed and leaned over for a peek out the porthole window that
overlooked the backyard. From beyond the peak of the roof,
she could see the merry tops of hollyhocks, almost spent for
the season, bobbing in the late morning light. She picked up
her phone and saw she'd slept until 10. That would be 8AM
LA time, she thought, three hours later than normal. She
and Aunt Carla stayed up talking and remembering until
late, when the older woman yawned and begged off to bed.
It had been a long time since she'd slept that hard, and she
felt slightly puffy and disoriented as she swung her legs over
the side of the bed, onto the hand-latched rug beneath her
feet.

She curled her toes into the soft snips of yarn and inhaled
deeply, taking in that particular set of scents that never
failed to bring back all her best childhood memories. There
was little love in her heart for Indiana, but the intensity
and specificity of its scent profile was special. The lawns,

whatever grass they grew up here, wasn't the St. Augustine or Bermuda varieties she knew from the south. This grass was tall and straight and green and smelled so sweet, so green when freshly mown. Blue spruce scattered fragrant terpenes on every breath of wind. The sweetness of a nearby corn field filled the place, a signature scent in the olfactory menagerie of Aunt Carla's House.

Though her aunt moved multiple times over the years as her fortunes waxed and waned, the scent of her followed and firmly embedded itself wherever she was. It was made of altar candles, and stacks of quilting fabrics still starched from the store. George breathed in, identifying each piece of the profile. Incense. Pine Sol. Dogs. Lilac aerosol spray, good black Indiana soil, clean laundry, coffee, and the mellow, flat scent of dried-up, ancient sticks – the steady bones of Aunt Carla's old farmhouse. Lavender and comfrey balm. Pink bar soap. White bread in a plastic bag. Other, more subtle nuances she couldn't identify. There was comfort in the immutability of the way Aunt Carla exerted her gentle presence upon a space. George thought brokenly that this could be the last time she might ever experience it, and she took it in slowly, trying to commit it to memory.

George pulled on a pair of leggings and a clean t-shirt and padded down the stairs in her sock feet as she gathered her hair into a bun. She rounded the bottom of the stairs, swinging around the banister at the end, and found herself face-to-face with two, wide-eyed, tow-headed boys. All three froze in place and stared at each other. The two looked like male versions of Hannah and her twin, Henry, at their ages. Jack, aged six. He had Hannah's shock of white hair, and her beautiful, porcelain-fine skin and blue eyes, the color of the deep sea. And Michael was eight, round-faced and sweet, with Henry's light blue eyes, stocky legs, button nose, sun-kissed skin, and a messy head of honey hair that appeared to be exclusively constructed of misbehaving cowlicks. They were staying with a friend of the family when George arrived, so this was her first time seeing them since Jack was in diapers.

A smile spread across George's face, and she softened, taking a knee to get to their level. "Michael," she reached out to shake his hand, and he looked pleased as he solemnly shook it. "I'm Georgia."

"Cousin Georgia?"

"That's me."

"All the way from California?"

She laughed and he smiled at her tentatively. "All the way from California." She turned to the other boy and extended her hand.

"Jack, it's nice to meet you again. The last time I saw you, you were a tiny baby." He looked up at her with his huge, haunted eyes and shuffled his feet. George gently took his hand and placed it in hers, adjusting his fingers correctly for a handshake, and whispered, "Just like that… right, now squeeze my hand a little and go up and down like this." A smile touched the corner of his mouth, then disappeared. "That's a good handshake."

She released his little fingers as Michael tugged her sleeve. "I would like to thank you for coming here for my mama's funeral," he said in a formal voice. Her smile faded and she touched his cheek.

"I'm sorry for your loss, honey."

"Me too." Michael clutched her sleeve more tightly.

"Me too," whispered little Jack. They remained there for a moment, looking at each other. George wasn't sure what to say, and the boys stared at her expectantly.

"What should we do? How can we honor the memory of your mama?"

Michael made a thoughtful face. "What's that mean?"

"We'd think up something that would have made your mama happy, and when we remember doing it, we'll have happy memories too."

"What if we plant flowers? Grammy did that when Uncle Henry died." George nodded.

"That's a good idea," she stalled, nodding slowly. She foresaw future trauma in leaving behind a memorial flower bed at a home that would soon be vacant, and she wasn't sure how much they knew about Aunt Carla's condition. "But what if…" She paused thoughtfully for a few beats.

"What?" Michael demanded.

"I was thinking we should go to the forest and plant a tree. If we plant a tree, it could grow for a hundred years. Long after this house is gone, and we're all gone, that tree can live in the forest. And that way it can be around friends, and forest creatures…"

"Forever?" asked Jack.

"Maybe," George shrugged. She thought to herself that no forest stood a chance against the encroachment that was coming.

"But we won't be able to see it all the time," countered Michael.

"But you'll know it's out there, won't you? And when you think of it, you'll be able to see it here," she tapped her head. The boy looked thoughtful as understanding dawned.

"Like mama?"

"Like that," she answered with a breaking heart.

"I think that would be nice," Michael said slowly.

"How about we go see what we have to do today, and we can schedule our tree project around it?" The boys nodded, and they grabbed on tightly to her hands, pulling her in the direction of the kitchen.

Aunt Carla sat at the familiar old table, her drugstore reading specs perched on the end of her nose, sipping coffee and filling out the daily crossword with a blue ballpoint. She had a dot of blue ink on her chin. Her aunt had always been inclined to heavy, rounded hips and a lush bosom, her belly thick with the weight of having borne two human beings into existence. Now she was nothing, light as a wisp, and deeply lined. Her teeth had been sacrificed to the chemotherapy treatments, and without her dentures, her lips retreated back into her mouth, leaving her looking like a classic crone from old fairytale books. It had only been four years since she'd last visited. Between then and now, Aunt Carla appeared to have aged thirty years, the spitting image of George's great grandmother, the last time she saw her before stomach cancer took her.

She smiled up at George from her seat, her pen hovering just above the mark already on her chin. She realized George was studying her. She gestured down at her body. "Messed up, ain't it? Chemo. That shit'll kill ya." She laughed, her chest wheezing, and ruffled Jack's hair.

"Why don't you boys go outside for a bit, let me an' cousin Georgie talk." The boys protested and she pushed Michael toward the door with a gentle swat to his bottom, and Jack followed. "Go find the dog," Carla called after them.

"Want some coffee?" She pointed to the coffee maker with a pink nail. "There's a cup or so left up there, and there's powder creamer on the counter. Sugar, too." George moved to the counter and pulled a mug down. Aunt Carla's lungs rattled as she coughed again.

"I want to talk to you about some things." Aunt Carla tucked her pen into her newspaper and folded it, pushing it away a few inches. She adjusted it until it was at a perfect angle to the edge of the place mat. She fingered the seam of the mat and looked up at Georgia with rheumy eyes. George leaned against the counter and sipped her coffee. Aunt Carla patted the table.

"Come on over here and set down."

George ran her fingers lightly over the grooves left by fifty years of homework completed on its surface as she rounded the table. Was this set of crosshatches an H? Did Hannah write her name at the top left of her math homework in this spot?

George settled into the chair across from her aunt.

"The thing is, Michael's got some serious issues, his kidneys, you know, 'cause of Hannah's condition when she was pregnant. He's on Medicaid. Hannah was gettin' a lotta benefits because of her situation."

Her condition. Her situation, George thought wearily, being that she was a multiple-times-convicted felon, disabled single mother, with untreated mental health issues, and serious substance use problems. She sighed heavily. Hannah never stood a chance.

"Well, we can deal with that. I have incredible insurance."

"And Jack, he'll be alright. It's good this happened when he was so little. But I think he's autistic. Or obsessive-compulsive,

I don't know. Somethin'. Maybe both." She threw Georgia a mischievous grin. "When I'm too tired to fold my laundry, I just throw it on the chair all messy-like and he puts it away for me."

They laughed. Georgia stopped first, fading into a moment as she fondly studied the crinkles at the corners of her aunt's eyes against the high apple cheeks they shared.

"That's terrible," she said with a smile.

"Eh, I take the breaks where I can get 'em these days." Aunt Carla shrugged. "He'll be alright. He's little. He's got the energy." She worried at the edge of the placemat. "Hannah was working the hotel by the airport, you know. Doing…" Carla gestured and made a pained face.

George cut her off. "I get it. It's okay."

Carla shook her head. "I tried, Georgia Lane, I did what I could, but I had to release that girl to make her own decisions. I had to, I couldn't bear it…" Her voice broke, and George slid over to a closer seat so she could comfort her. She covered Aunt Carla's cold, pale hand with her warm and vital one.

"All my babies are gone. All I got's them boys." She sniffed back tears. "They never got their vaccines, Georgie. She read some whackjob shit on the internet and figured out how to get a religious exemption for school. Michael needs therapy, we got some issues, there."

"We'll work everything out. We have resources. It's going to be okay." She squeezed her aunt's hands. "You don't need to worry, not now."

There were arrangements that still needed to be made, invoices that needed paying, death certificates to pick up, catering, flowers, and a tree to be planted. Hannah's apartment needed cleaning out.

Then they talked about what would happen when Aunt Carla died. She made George promise to go through her crates of photos. She'd always been the de facto family photographer, and now she worried about whether or not everyone would get the right ones when she was gone. They talked funeral and end-of-life logistics until the boys tumbled in, sweaty and yelling, with Sandy the dog. It was both familiar and surreal to be doing this again. It left little room for grieving.

George knew exactly how to handle this part of death. As long as there were tasks, everything would be fine. Being competent was her highest competence.

Saudade

(n.) The feeling of missing something so deeply that it's almost a presence in itself.

The day of the funeral dawned uncharacteristically hot, humid, and gray for early fall, and George was already sweating in her black sheath dress by the time they arrived at the home. She staged the flowers and the guestbook, laid out the food, and delegated with an air of authority that made early arrivals think she was part of the staff.

Hannah's funeral was a blur. Everyone wanted to greet George, express sympathy and share memories while she struggled to display the right level of pleasant sympathy. She managed not to cry more than a few dignified slips that she carefully dabbed away without consequence to her eye makeup. She kept the color from rising in her face and her nose didn't run. She considered it some sort of victory against death. Not the war. But certainly, a battle.

George excused herself from the frigid communal room and slipped out a service entrance, into the enveloping humidity. She leaned against the building and sighed in relief. Hidden from view behind a potted evergreen, she perched on the edge of the planter. Someone had stashed a pack of cigarettes between the tree and the wall. She went down on her heels and retrieved it, then popped the cardboard lid back. Half a pack and a Bic lighter. Fuck it. She rose, peeked around the branches to make sure she was alone, then savored half of one stolen cigarette before stubbing it out in the dirt and stashing the pack back in its hiding place. She rinsed her mouth and hands in the bathroom and looked into the mirror. A familiar stranger stared back at her. She felt disconnected from her body, buzzed from the cigarette. She walked on wooden legs back into the fray.

Her disjointed thoughts spun wildly, but she somehow managed to interact normally enough that no one remarked on her behavior. At some point, a soft little hand clutched hers and held on, then disappeared, gone to join the other cousins. Someone touched her shoulder lightly and inserted a cup of coffee into her hand. She gripped it like a lifeline. A woman she didn't remember asked whatever happened after she moved out to California. Said she remembered how George used to play guitar and had the prettiest voice. *Did you ever get famous?* she asked. The questions, the open curiosity, hearing the stories Hannah told everyone about her. Their words jumbled up into a salad that would haunt her sleep for the rest of the year.

By that night, though, she wouldn't remember any of their faces.

That night, George slept like the dead.

5

Faeloria

(n.) The beauty that grows from wounds you thought
would destroy you.

George sipped her coffee and swung gently on the weathered swing, set beneath a willow arch twined with roses. The sun rose into the quiet blue morning, and the pale mist lifted from the grass. Birds called out, so many more bird sounds than she ever heard in the city limits. She whispered that she'd love a breeze and almost laughed when a curl of wind spun up, as if on command, and kissed her cheeks. Aunt Carla convinced her when she was little that she could control the wind if she asked it the right way, and it was some great mystery of the Universe for George that it always worked.

By the time Aunt Carla and the boys were up, George's work gear and overnight bag were packed into the rental. She gave hugs and kisses, then pulled out in a slow crunch of gravel until she was back on the country road.

She set her GPS, stopped for gas, and picked a good road trip playlist as she waited for the tank to fill. She pulled out onto the highway, kachunk over the pitted concrete entrance, broken by the weight of too many big rigs, and hit 31N. The long, black ribbon and the blessed promise of five-and-a-half-hours of silence unfolded before her.

Even though it was impossible not to think about the fraught circumstances of her visit, it was equally impossible not to feel the lightness of her solitude. Pain rose and fell in her chest as her mind, alighted gently on various memories. She did not have to suppress anything in this little fiberglass bubble that cradled her as it hurtled through time and space. She thought of the photo she kept near her desk: her grandparents, dad, Aunt Carla, Henry and Hannah before all their babies were born, and Aunt Carla's last set of dogs, Rocko and Bruiser. That was a good day. She and dad stayed up until sunrise, creeping quietly to bed before Grandma woke.

It was the height of a green Indiana summer in the photo, the way it always was in her mind. It felt odd to be here in the autumn. After forty-four years of existence in this eternal-summer place, it felt like forbidden knowledge to witness the moving of seasons that had been denied her.

That night was the last one she spent with her dad, and she was sure, in retrospect, that he'd been planning it even then. All the signs were there: the wistful way his fingers caught at hers as they parted at the airport the next day; sharing the family stories that only he knew, explaining why he felt the world had become too mean. He tried to prepare her.

She turned into a puddle on the kitchen floor when Grandpa called her, three days out from her first National tour. *We've already fixed the RV,* she argued. *There are shows booked, and we had to leave on Wednesday. There's no way I can make it back for the funeral.* Grandpa slowed and soothed her with calm words. She could hear that he was crying. That really scared the shit out of her.

You'll come back, it's gonna be okay, Georgia. Come be with your family.

When she hung up, she collapsed onto the linoleum and cried so hard she vomited on the floor and heaved until there was nothing left. Later, she cleaned the kitchen until her hands cracked and bled. That was the night she poured a pint of vodka over ice and began drinking in earnest.

Now, Aunt Carla was the last living person in the memento of that last day George had with her dad. She would be gone soon, too.

It was one of those years, 2005, where every damn thing went wrong. It started with a literal bang when her best friend from childhood died by suicide. Stress was at an all-time high as she and Pete prepared for the tour, all their money sunk into a failing RV that didn't want to be fixed. Her apartment was robbed, her guitar stolen. The engineer who was producing their album pulled a coke-fueled disappearing trick before he turned over the masters. Hurricane Katrina devastated Louisiana. Her father gave up his ghost willingly, and her cousin Jordan was taken by a trigger-happy cop. The deadly Indonesian tsunami would be a parting gift of that cursed year. Start-to-finish, it had been an entire piece of shit.

George thought about the trajectory she'd taken after that phone call. The hard drinking, the touring, the damn-the-torpedoes approach to everything. She and her best friend in a van, blowing up their relationship and the band in one fell swoop, going to live with her pre-Kato boyfriend back in New York, blowing up *that* relationship, wandering the East Coast aimlessly for a year, playing shows to empty bars, then moving back to LA with her tail between her legs.

After that, tragedy in her inner circle seemed to follow in

her wake with a relentlessness that exhausted her. Over the next fifteen years she would lose tens of friends to suicides and overdoses. Running in professional artist circles didn't help.

Had it not been for a strong dose of luck and a chance meeting that put her in the same room as Lucia, she wasn't sure what her life would look like now.

The sun was high in the sky before she stopped to top off the tank and stretch her legs.

Her mind drifted to Ben Macon. She wasn't sure what she was thinking when she accepted Lucia's little side quest. Aside from generally just being a complete asshole, there was a sizeable list in her head of all the bad things she knew about him. He'd hurt her best friend, Melly, so badly she put a gun in her mouth after the breakup. Before she died, Melly told her about all the ways he emotionally abused her, gaslit her, and, in the end, physically accosted her before he finally left for good. There was no way George would be able to feel safe in his presence, knowing what he did. And now she was headed for his cabin. The confidence she felt in LA when she accepted, thinking she wouldn't have trouble keeping it business, had waned significantly as she had time to think about what she was actually doing. But she was in it now. The worst outcome she could think of was that she'd end up spending her night in the car before returning to Indy and reporting back to Lucia that it was a bust. She'd manage. She always did. That didn't mean it wasn't the height of stupidity for her to have accepted.

She was north of Chicago, now, and despite only being three hours north of Indy, the air was much crisper, sharper;

autumn was well underway in this neck of the woods. The blushing deciduous trees slowly made way to straight-trunk-ed, tall pines. She shivered as she inhaled the clean air. To the north, a bank of dark storm clouds gathered. She shook out her legs once more and got back into the car. Just an hour and change left. She was glad she'd be arriving while it was light, ahead of the storm. Some of those roads leading out to the rental looked fairly rustic from the satellite view.

When the pavement was once again humming beneath her wheels, she replayed her fortuitous meeting with Lucia.

A friend of a friend, whom she'd been considering seducing, invited her to a birthday soiree for his Hollywood accountant. The accountant, Louise, was a fabulous elderly woman with wild, permed white hair, long red nails, a be-dazzled kaftan, and the best wine collection George had ever been invited to drink. And, in the way many of those cliched Hollywood discovery stories started, George found herself being discovered by the type of person you want to have on your side when you need to make connections. Louise took a shine to George. That night, they stood in the wine closet of the penthouse condo overlooking a particu-larly bougie stretch of Ventura Blvd and talked for an hour, before Louise squinted thoughtfully at her.

"There are some people I want to introduce you to," she said, and took George's hand. She led her back into the party and introduced Lucia as a "fellow music aficionado." Had George known who the woman was, she might not have been able to speak. Louise was a collector of people – artists, specifically. George found herself fast-tracked into the collection for reasons unbeknownst to her.

She realized with a start that she'd met Kato for the first

time that night, too. Why hadn't she remembered that? It was him, she thought with a frown, who was standing with Lucia when Louise introduced them. "And this is Kato Kamata, an absolutely brilliant installation artist." Louise surreptitiously pushed them a little closer to each other.

That was the first of three times she would meet Kato before she remembered who he was – and before he found George interesting, he'd confessed. The second was at one of his art openings, and she was in a bad place with a bad guy at the time.

They spent three years orbiting each other before managing to get the timing right. When they finally came together just a few weeks after their third introduction, it was a lightning bolt. They were so impulsive in those days. The first night of their many nights together, at George's 5th Annual Outlaw Christmas Convening, the mutual friend Kato came with left without saying goodbye, throwing George a knowing smile as he slipped out the front door.

She sent the rest of the guests home. Alone and giddy with sexual tension, they killed the better part of a case of craft brew and cracked a bottle of Dewars by the firepit. At some point, he stood and casually tossed his whiskey glass to the ground behind him and muttered fuck it, as he moved forward and yanked her up into his arms and a kiss. She was so startled by the shattering glass she hardly had time to in-tellectually register that he was holding her. Her body knew what to do right away; she leaned into him and greedily tore at his clothes as she dragged him, very willingly, into the bedroom.

And that was it; they were never apart after that.

Somewhere along the line, early on, even, she and Kato

became best friends and stopped being lovers.

Her last night back in LA, he did all the loving things for her: packed her bag while she worked late, made dinner, kneaded into her sore neck and back with skilled hands, and kissed her sweetly on the temple as he whispered words of support. She couldn't imagine a better partner in life.

But he didn't react when she mentioned she'd be gone the entirety of September. Their anniversary fell at the end of the month, too. Apparently, the idea of her spending a few days in a cabin with a strange man didn't faze him in the slightest.

He didn't notice when she put on her sexiest bra and tight tank top and leaned against him as he navigated streaming channels to find a movie. Nor when she stroked his beauti-fully formed, long runner's legs with their light dusting of curly hair with a firm, slow palm, where their limbs folded together on the couch. Even though she willed him to see her and nibbled his ear. He made happy sounds and pulled her closer, then leaned in sideways to plant an awkward kiss on her cheek, his eyes glued to his phone screen and whatever news he was engrossed in. That night when they finally retired, though they rarely touched in bed, she cuddled up close to him, spooning her bottom into the curve of his legs, and he'd fallen asleep stroking her hair, leaving her wanting.

She probably could have had him there on the couch. He wouldn't have denied her. He rarely denied her anything. But she wanted something more than pleasant acquies-cence. She wanted him to tear her apart. She wanted it with a hard, violent, dark desperation that set her teeth on edge. What she wanted was his *need*.

She wanted to feel any-fucking-thing.

She just wasn't sure how to fix that now. Consumed with her thoughts, she slammed her palms against the steering wheel and let loose a wordless scream of frustration. Lightning cut through the sky above, so near that the thunder rolled out before the light faded.

A heavy raindrop smashed against her windshield and spread outward into tight tendrils. The stiff wind whipped up and shivered the pines, buffeting her car lightly. Darkness descended as she drove into the storm.

Two hours later, she pulled over to the shoulder of a dirt road. Her phone finally stopped connecting to her navigation app forty-five minutes ago, and she'd been trying to navigate the dark road on her memory of the directions since then, which she should have known was a terrible idea. Now night was upon her, and the rain was coming down in heavy sheets. She sighed and looked around. She was stuck in the car, on this road, at least for the duration of the storm. The thought of having to spend the night in damp clothes was enough to keep her from trying to get out and stretch her stiff legs, even for a second.

She craned her neck to look up, but all she could see were wildly dancing, dark branches that caught the impotent glow of her headlights. She heaved another resigned sigh and turned them off. She turned off her phone to save the battery and leaned back in her seat. She sat alone in the dark, with the rain and wind rocking her lightly. Despite her surety that she'd lay awake all night, she fell asleep quickly.

She was alone outside an A-frame building, warmly stained wood with black trim, gold light blazing from the edifice of glass that looked out on the desert mountain pass. Mist obscured the valley below, and the cliffs above, and the road ahead and behind. Shredded clouds hurried past and wrapped the building, tatters of gray on gray. Silence weighted the air, the mist dampening all the sounds, except for the sharp crunch of gravel underfoot. Tall cliffs jutted up darkly, background to the building that seemed to grow straight out of the mountainside, rock and pine plank melting into one another in sharp, illogical edges and corners. She looked for her mother; she could hear her muffled voice inside. She looked down and she was five again, her little bare toes dug into the gravel of the roadside. She wore the long, white nightgown with little, blue flowers, with a ruffle around the neck and sleeves. It was her favorite, and when she wore it, she pretended she was a princess. When she was seven, she would be involved in a bloody, early-morning accident that would stain a full side of the white fabric. After that, it wasn't long for the world. Mom let her throw it on the solstice bonfire. The garment's lower ruffle would reach the middle of her shins by then. But here, now, she was still five, and the ruffle brushed along the ground as she moved toward the gallery's wide front doors.

She remembered this dream, and in it, knew she was dreaming. Now she would hear her mother's voice in the upper gallery of the A-frame building. Her mother never worked here, it was merely a construct made sharper by the lack of life experiences at the age she first had this nightmare. The floating, ambiguous terror as she dutifully mounted the stairs. Climbing deep steps of knotted, golden pine, one by one. The rich smells of the bins of wood moulding, rolls of paper, wood putty encasing her. The exertion of climbing the too-high steps. She would climb to the top and search the gallery, but she would never home in on her mother's exact location, her laughing voice always just beyond reach, her words just beyond comprehension. She would sit down in the corner of the landing and watch the front door at the bottom of the tall staircase, to make sure her mother couldn't leave without her, and when she finally fell asleep in the corner of the landing, she would wake up. It was always the same. She didn't know the point of this dream, but she'd been having it for forty years.

For the first time, a new element was introduced. As she grew sleepy on the cold landing, the bell over the door jingled. George stood and peered over the rail of the stairs to see her Aunt Carla, standing motionless inside the entry.

"It's time to die, Georgia Lane. Time to be reborn." She lifted her face and looked at George, with black, yawning holes where her eyes should be. "Come," she said, and her mouth widened into a gaping abyss. George's stomach flipped as she fell over the railing, and into her aunt's mouth.

6

Waldeinsamkeit

(n.) The serene, reflective state one finds in the quiet and
isolation of the natural world, away from the bustle of
urban life.

George opened her eyes. For a moment, she thought
she was still falling through that black expanse. The
rain had stopped. She cracked the car door experimentally
and found the air still, leaving only the quiet sounds of a
dripping forest. She gasped at the cold when she stepped
out to stretch her legs. She leaned into the backseat to grab
a hoodie from the overnight bag and frowned; she'd need
to go shopping for a proper coat if she was going to be up
here at the end of the month. She pulled the sweatshirt over
her head and turned on her phone while she looked at her
surroundings in the low light that shone from the inside of
the car.

An owl warbled a soft question somewhere close by. Otherwise, it was profoundly quiet. She pulled in deep breaths
of the cold, clean air. *Heaven.* As she waited for her phone
to finish starting up, she looked up through the trees and
delighted in the multitude of bright stars that were visible,
a hum of appreciation in her throat. The wind stirred, and
died, sending a fresh pattering of droplets onto the forest
floor.

The phone finally initialized and she held it up in the air. No signal. She crossed the muddy road carefully and stood on a higher bank. No signal. She exhaled in frustration. It was 2AM, the darkest part of the night, the moon sleeping somewhere out of reach. She'd be here for another four hours, at least, waiting for enough light to start driving again. She stood in the center of the road, looking backward, and then ahead. She didn't feel tired. It would be terrible to sit in the cramped vehicle that long. She chewed the inside of her cheek and wondered if there were bears and cougars up here. *Fuck it.*

She stayed on the wide country road and walked in the direction she'd been driving. As long as she kept the car in sight, she'd be fine. *Drip,* a drop of water tapped a leaf as it fell. She registered the quiet crackling of rainwater filtering through the gravelly soil. The tiny gentle noises surrounded her. *The trees are drinking,* she thought, and lost herself in discovering the subtle noises of the forest as she walked. Before long she hit a curve in the road and stopped. There was only one way to go; it wasn't as if she could get lost. As soon as there was an intersection of any kind where she could get her bearing, she would turn back. But for now, the road was singular in its path, and she looked back at the little car back down the way, weighing the risk of continuing. There was no harm, and the night was exhilarating.

Crackle. Drip. The wet crunch of her step in the road. She continued. The last of the clouds parted and a bright half-moon appeared, illuminating the road, and the shadows of branches undulated softly across its surface, deepening into the forest. She walked in silence, feeling her blood warm, her muscles loosen. A gust of wind blew a spray of droplets across her cheek. She luxuriated in the sharp, snow-kissed scent of the cold rainwater.

She followed several natural curves in the road before hitting a straightaway. Ahead, the road stretched out until it disappeared into the darkness. She looked at her phone: she'd been walking for over an hour. She decided to turn back, a little crestfallen at not having found a street sign of any kind. She stifled a yawn and turned around. At least, she thought, she'd probably be worn out enough to sleep through the rest of the night when she got back to the car. She wasn't looking forward to cramping herself back into that seat.

Forty-four found her with very specific requirements when it came to sleeping arrangements. Those requirements were born of a bad back and an utter refusal to compromise that particular comfort. After spending a great deal of her formative years and young adulthood sleeping on camping mats, in cars, couches, subway seats and various booths in uncountable bars, she felt sleeping comfortably had been earned.

In her late twenties, how many nights had she and Pete slept in the van as they crept from bar to bar and city to city? With a van full of merch, amps, and instruments, they'd scarcely had room to lay out straight, bracketed by hard gear, stacked as neatly as possible: mic stands and hard cases, all the unforgiving accoutrement of music-making which were never meant to be invited into bed. Back then, it was exhilarating, but she was too old and tired for that shit now.

Their meandering path took them on a steady north-east trajectory until they finally landed in New York. They

hustled on construction sites, and sold jewelry, scarves —
and whatever else anyone wanted them to peddle — in the
holiday market at Columbus Circle. They played shows six
nights a week, and book-ended their nights going to other
bands' shows. The level of talent one could stumble upon in
some shabby New York dive bar was unfathomable. They
landed, through sheer force of luck and some fortuitously
gained contacts, temporary digs in a Hell's Kitchen penthouse. They drank coffee in white and blue paper cups and
munched ninety-nine cent slices as they walked over the
Brooklyn Bridge, dragging their gear behind them when a
transit strike stopped all the trains. They reveled in the effortless acquisition of gigs and residencies. They played ev-
erywhere. No one bought the merch. But the people came.
*Not like LA, where you can't give away a mixtape and everything is
pay-to-play.* She pursed her lips and silently thanked herself
for the one thousandth time, for giving up that side of music.

She retraced her path, following the curve, and began to
take the next curve to the left, when she realized she was at
a fork in the road. She squinted into the shadows in both
directions. Somehow, she'd missed this in the darkness, as
the fork would have veered off behind her, and now that she
was standing face to face with the choice, she wasn't sure
which way she should go. All the shadows had shifted since
she started, and she had been too deeply lost in her thoughts
to pay attention to the path.

She looked back and tried to judge how long ago she'd
walked past the last bend in the road. George tentatively
took a step toward the right path, which curved off around a
concealing corner. The moonlight turned everything watery
and unfamiliar. The wind gave a little gust and she hugged

her hoodie tightly against her, and she was confronted with the magnitude of the situation.

She was alone. In the woods. With no phone signal, and not enough clothes to protect her. *Fuck.* She didn't know anything about this area and wasn't sure if continuing down these pathways would lead her further from her destination. She might walk for miles only to find herself in the heart of this forest, which, she thought with a shudder, could conceivably reach almost to Canada. On the other hand – the wind gusted again and she shivered, now with both fear and cold – she couldn't do nothing at all. She stepped onto the right-hand path and began to walk. Maybe she'd get lucky.

George had always been lucky. She thought so, anyway.

She was born to two teenagers into an era where "family planning" in such a situation either involved a shotgun wedding or a "trip out west" to birth and rehome the child under a cloak of anonymity. They opted for the wedding, and several months later, George was born and baptized quickly, lest the wickedness that spawned her corrupt her immortal soul. She was a sickly baby and was born into the most furious blizzard to hit the Midwest in a century, as the old-timers liked to remember. So, she was lucky to be alive, for starters.

The marriage didn't last long. Mom followed Dad to Houston where they tried to start a new life and instead found new temptations and ruin. That was when they started moving. She remembered being small and waiting for her father to come pick her up – for Christmas, for AstroWorld, for a lunch out. He never showed. But it certainly his doing that, on a particularly lean Christmas, five

Hell's Angels, smelling of leather and motor oil and wearing matching riding jackets, showed up with a small, freshly cut Christmas tree, wrapped presents, and several bags of food. They always seemed to scrape by somehow.

They lived in her mom's giant, 1979 Volaré when they got to Texarkana. When they arrived in the middle of the night, they ate cornflakes and water in the car and slept fitfully under the bright yellow sodium lights that rimmed the dam at the county line. After that, they parked in various dark neighborhoods, not so wealthy that someone would call the police, but not so poor it would be loud at night. Though they lived in a variety of precarious conditions and risky situations, nothing bad ever really happened to them except for George's tendency to get frequently and seriously ill. But it was her frequent illnesses that caused a sympathetic clinic doctor to take pity on her mom and let them stay in the converted garage for free until she got on her feet. If that wasn't luck, she didn't know what was.

Each workday that winter, her mom left George nestled in the spacious floor of the Volaré's backseat under a blanket, while she worked the perfume counter at Dillard's department store. *Don't let anyone see you. Don't unlock the doors,* she said to George, *or people will come to take you away.* George stayed under the blanket and kept herself busy with her Barbie and endless hours of imaginary adventures. She considered herself lucky that she hadn't been taken out of her mother's care.

She would find, as a young adult, that she was lucky at games of chance. After her first fortuitous trip to Vegas for a bachelorette party, she slowly gained a reputation for attracting luck. It sounded absurd, but she simply knew things.

She felt it most keenly with dice. She could whisper the combination of dice at the craps table while her partner threw out chips in the appropriate squares with 95% accuracy. She actually had no idea of how the game was played. A foggy framework existed, but she was so focused on the actual dice that she didn't understand all the details. On more than one occasion, they'd been at the center of a hot table, people following the lead of her partner's bets and causing a furious uproar with each successful throw. Big enough to attract the pit boss's stern attention.

Rich men, the fathers of her LA friends, took her on weekend trips for the sole purpose of playing psychic arm candy. She didn't have to do a thing but make them rich, and she was treated to slinky designer gowns and private suites where she and her friends could order room service before hitting the late-night spots. These older guys liked to think they were mobsters, and they wanted their lady to look the part. And to their credit, not a single one of them ever tried anything untoward. She happily obliged for the perks.

And luckiest of all, perhaps, she didn't inherit whatever chemical or genetic aberration most of her family had; that tendency toward addiction and some lack of fortitude that made them prone to giving up. She had problem times, for sure. Drinking too much. Doing… everything too much. Imagining how much easier it would be to clap out.

But her survival instinct was strong. It wasn't hard to change her behavior, once she decided she really wanted to. She simply poured herself obsessively into work. Always work, and then nothing else could breach the weak spots in her armor. She was lucky she could still have a single drink once in a blue moon or smoke a little pot without repercussions. She chose not to, but she *could*. And that made her different than dad, Hannah, Henry, and Melly, and… all the rest. She knew inhabiting her body this way was a privilege. Intellectually, she did. But she couldn't help being blindingly angry with every one of them for not being able to get their shit together before it killed them. Angry and hurt that they chose their vices instead of staying there with her. For leaving her behind to deal with all their big, fucking messes.

She loved them with her whole heart and missed them all so desperately, still. And she hated them, too.

George paused in the road, which had narrowed to not much more than a rutted and weed-choked path. She turned her phone on and looked at the time. She should have been back to the car by now. She was definitely in the wrong place. She stopped and tried to think through a course of action, but she was so tired, and so cold. She backtracked until she found the fork in the road and tried to visualize what direction she'd gone. She oriented herself as she walked back to the main road, looking back at the path she'd just come from. *Yes, this is the one,* she decided confidently.

She hoped her lifelong relationship with Lady Luck was in good standing. Inside her hoodie pocket, she crossed her cold fingers. She walked down the left-hand fork in the road as the moon dipped below the horizon. The wind began to blow in more forcefully from the north. The night clutched onto the darkness and it was no longer charming. She sat down beneath the shelter of three large pines and slid to the ground with a sigh of relief. She just needed to rest her feet briefly, and then she'd continue.

Maybe I'll start a fire.

But instead, she shut her eyes for just a second and fell asleep.

Foudroyant

(adj.) Like a lightning strike; something sudden, over-whelming, dazzling, or devastating.

George yawned and snuggled more deeply into the warm blanket that cocooned her, consciousness slowly dawning. The fabric of the cover smelled delicious and un-familiar, like winter spices and pine resin, campfire smoke. Something else, too. Someone else. Someone masculine. A fire crackled nearby, and the air was redolent with the warming scent of coffee. She dozed, idly considering this puzzle.

Suddenly she woke fully and sat up straight. *Where the hell am I?*

She clutched the comforter to her chest and realized she was wearing a large, unfamiliar sweater, and no pants.

OH, GOD.

George racked her brain, trying to remember how she'd gotten here. "Hello?" She called tentatively and heard someone stir in another part of the house? *Cabin.* She was in a cabin. Currently in a small bedroom with a good-sized bed, and a little wood dresser with a single lamp. No adorn-ment. Raw wood walls, and there was a black potbelly stove visible through the door. She stood and was relieved to see the sweater fell to her knees. She padded toward the door on thick, white tube socks that weren't hers, either. Through it, a spacious living room opened up to the rafters of the tall, vaulted ceiling. To her left, a closed door, painted forest green, from which sounds of movement issued. A caramel-colored couch that had seen better days was set against one wall with a plain coffee table before it. A broom rested upright in a corner. A loft area rose over a small kitchen, separated from the main room by a waist-high bar, two tall stools tucked neatly under its overhang. Another door to the left of the fridge, and on the adjoining wall, windows looking out into a glen surrounded by trees, and the front door. A tidy little place, with a battered tin carafe of green pine branches arranged on a four-seater kitchen table, but otherwise austere. She stood in the warmth of a sunbeam that shone through the window.

"Hello."

George spun to meet the deep voice that greeted her and found herself a few feet away from a very tall, very broad man leaning against the door jamb of the room next to hers, cradling a steaming cup of coffee in his large hands. Her eyes traveled up from the cup in his hands, nearly at her eye level, across the wide chest of a red flannel button down, and flitted up to his face, taking in his long, mountain-man beard. It covered so much of his face that she couldn't tell how old he was. Maybe thirty, maybe fifty. He was massive. She took a half-step back as she met his piercing blue eyes, which regarded her with an intensity that set her off kilter. There was something so familiar about those eyes. He sipped his coffee languidly and continued to look at her.

"How did I get here?" George finally managed, after spending an agonizing several seconds trying to find her words.

"I found you in the woods."

"What do you mean, you found me in the woods?"

"Just as I said. I was walking a back road, and I found you under a tree, like a wee changeling." He wasn't smiling but wore a look of friendly curiosity. "What were you doing way out here?"

She frowned, and her forehead crinkled as she tried to remember.

"You would have been in serious trouble if I hadn't stumbled over you. I tripped on one of those——" He motioned to the hot pink athletic shoes near the potbelly stove. "I don't know if I would have noticed you otherwise." Near the chimney, wood clothespins held her socks over the stove from a string that was suspended from opposite corners of the nearby wall. "You wouldn't wake up."

She blinked at him, still trying to clear the cobwebs of sleep out of her brain.

"So, I brought you here," He finished simply, and swallowed more coffee. He held up his cup. "Want some? You seemed slightly more wakeful when I checked on you an hour ago, so I made extra."

"*Wait*," Georgia demanded, "Are you saying you carried me here?"

"Yes." He regarded her calmly.

"How far?" Her brain worked madly, trying to reclaim what time she'd lost. She struggled against a blooming sense of alarm, in which she imagined this brawny stranger slinging her over one shoulder and carrying her through the woods. *Who* did *that? Why didn't he call the authorities?*

He laughed quietly at the question, and she had a feeling

she was asking all the wrong things. "Does it get me extra points if I say it was miles upon miles, in the midst of a furious tempest?" His smile faded as he saw her expression. "About two-thousand feet. And it was sprinkling?" he offered.

"I don't understand," she began to say, when in fact, she did understand, as she suddenly remembered the entire thing all at once. The nighttime journey, the fork in the road, the rest by the tree. Even the little flits in and out of consciousness as this man carried her through the soggy woods. She realized with a blush, which started at her knees and continued into the ether when it reached her crown, he hadn't slung her over his shoulder at all; he'd cradled her like a baby in his arms. Christ on a stick. She looked away in embarrassment.

"I got lost," she muttered lamely.

"No doubt," he agreed. "Coffee?"

She tried to regain her dignity and somehow found the wherewithal to meet his eyes with a weak smile. "I'd love some."

George tucked herself into one end of the squishy couch and folded her legs underneath her. She arranged the sweater strategically so she wasn't flashing any unnecessary body parts at the large man who settled into the opposite end of the sofa. He watched as she took a sip. Warmth flooded her body and she closed her eyes.

"Dear god, that's good. Thank you…" She paused. "Shit. I'm so sorry, but what is your name?" Now that she was more awake, all the questions she should have asked before rushed into her brain.

He looked at her oddly before he finally spoke. "My friends

call me Trip," he said, and then added, "I guess you can call me that, too." His face remained passive, but she realized he was messing with her.

"I'm George. There's no way I can thank you enough." She shook her head and allowed her shoulders to drop. If he'd wanted to hurt her, he'd already had ample opportunity, and she wasn't getting weird vibes from him. "Since we're friends in the making, I wonder, ahhh… if you could tell me…" She gestured at the sweater with a rueful look. "I seem to be missing some of the things I arrived in. I'd like to know exactly what happened after you found me."

His eyebrows shot up, his blue eyes widened, and she saw his body push into the couch, away from her. He held both hands up as if to say, don't shoot. "I didn't touch you, I swear," he said seriously. "I mean − I did touch you. I had to touch you… but only where I had to − to get your clothes off." Her eyes narrowed and he paused. "Fuck me, that was terrible, wasn't it? How about I start over and don't mention touching you ten times in a row? That made me sound like a creep."

"That would be a good start." She couldn't help feeling amused by his flustered state.

"I found you in the woods. You were freezing and soaked from head to toe. I carried you here. I undressed you in the dark." He paused and gave her a sheepish look. "It was *nearly* dark. The sun was coming up, but I didn't turn on any lights. I tried only to look when I needed to − for purposes of not accidentally strangling you with the neck of that sweater, for instance."

She nodded and encouraged him to continue.

"I didn't take off any of your undergarments," he said

bluntly. "I didn't think you'd appreciate that even though they were wet. Besides, there wasn't enough to them to qualify as a problem." He realized what he'd revealed as soon as the words left his mouth, and looked away from her, suddenly very interested in rubbing a spot off the handle of his mug.

She decided to let it go. No use in punishing this nice lumberjack who probably saved her life. "Alright," she conceded as she finished her coffee. "That's good enough for me. That's an acceptable reason for why I'm naked. I think I would like my pants back, though."

He visibly relaxed. "You're hardly *naked*." On her withering look, he raised his hands up again. "Maybe this is the wrong time to argue that point." He stood and brushed his hands down his legs. "I shall retrieve the lady's pants, which should be dry by now. Then we can have some food and figure out what to do." She nodded gratefully and realized she was starving. He moved toward the ladder and hoisted himself up with three long pulls of his powerful arms. She studied his brawny form, and compared it to Kato's graceful, thin body in her head.

"Oh my god!" She exclaimed and popped to her feet. *What the hell is wrong with me? Kato.* "I need my phone! Where is it?"

Trip turned, one hand still grasping the ladder and his other clutching a handful of her clothes. Her jeans looked like children's clothes in his giant paw. He gave her a quizzical look. "I found you with nothing but the clothes on your back."

"What time is it?"

He hopped down a couple rungs, and then onto the floor. He approached and handed over her clothing, then walked to the window and looked out for a second. "2:30 in the afternoon." She did a double take and wondered if he was actually telling time just by looking outside.

"Okay, okay." A string of thoughts flashed through her mind. She grouped them neatly into an actionable list in the correct order to get her back on track. "You said you found me about two-thousand feet from here?" He nodded. "Perfect. Would you mind showing me?"

He grunted. She tried awkwardly to pull on her jeans and wriggle into her shirt under the protective cover of the sweater.

"I'll give you some privacy," he murmured, and disappeared into the room from which he'd originally emerged. He shut the door softly behind him. She realized she was acting like a disaster and made a mental note to get her shit together.

Together they walked back to the tree where Trip discovered her. She wondered at how different, how much less wild, it looked on the road by daylight. It was a chilly, but benignly pleasant afternoon, a whiff of wood fire smoke scenting the piney air. The sun was already angling toward the horizon when they came upon the trio of pines where he found her. They skimmed their hands through the thick, wet mat of pine needles near the base of the tree in ever-widening circles. Her fingers touched something hard, and she squealed in triumph when she lifted her sodden phone, muddy and covered in detritus from the forest floor. A crack in the glass screen ran from one corner to the other, and she sighed. She began to press the power button, and he snatched it from her.

"Don't turn it on!"

She looked at him in disbelief. "Give me my phone."

He handed it back. "Sorry. Don't turn it on," he repeated. "We need to dry it out first, or you could ruin it."

She looked at it doubtfully. "Does it look… un-ruined enough to dry out?" She turned the device over in her hands.

He shrugged, but he didn't look optimistic. "Wouldn't hurt to try. I have some white rice and a couple silica packs back at the cabin."

She stood up from where she rested on her haunches. "Okay. I guess."

They ate cans of stew warmed up on the potbelly stove in comfortable silence. She poked at her phone, which sat on the table with their food, buried in rice.

"How long does this take?"

"Best leave it overnight," he said, "If it doesn't work in the morning, it probably won't ever."

"By morning?" she made a horrified face. "It's been twenty-fours since I checked in, people are going to be worried."

He paused with his spoon halfway to his mouth and stared at her for a long second. "You were out for two days, friend."

She gasped audibly. "No, no, no," she whispered. "Please – let me use your phone. There are people I need to talk to urgently."

"I'm sorry, I can't…"

A look of disbelief dawned on her face and she cut him off. "Look, whatever you need, Trip. If there are extra charges – I'll pay. Hell, I'll buy you a whole new phone. I don't care, I just need to touch base with work, and—"

"I don't have a phone," he interrupted. He spooned

another bite of stew calmly into his mouth.

She looked at him as though he'd just sprouted a second head. "You don't… have a… a mobile, or…? What do you mean? You have to have a phone number, *people just don't…*" she sputtered. "How do you even communicate up here?"

He shrugged. "I came here seeking peace, and I didn't feel like bringing distractions. I control who has access to my time," he said pointedly, ending the conversation.

She could hardly believe her ears. This was a nightmare. She'd been out for two days, and hadn't spoken with Lucia, Kato, Aunt Carla, or even Ben Macon. *Jesus.* She'd managed to drop every ball simultaneously. She rubbed the bridge of her nose and tried to gather herself.

"Well, I have to find a phone," she said in her most reasonable voice, despite the panic rising in her chest. "Surely there's one somewhere nearby, even if you don't have one. A store. A post office, a neighbor, even."

He shook his head. "Nope." He shoveled another big bite of stew into his mouth.

"You're telling me there's not a phone within driving distance of this cabin?"

"Not tonight, there's not," he said around the mouthful of stew. He gestured at the inky, black window. "I'll get you back to your car in the morning."

What is this man playing at? Panic rose in her chest. She didn't know anything about him. She slammed both hands down on the table a little harder than she meant to, causing him to jerk slightly before arranging a bland look on his face.

"Why are you doing this?" she demanded.

"What?" He raised his eyebrows. "What am I doing?"

She glowered at him. "Why won't you help me?"

He looked at her with an implacable expression and chewed in silence with his eyebrows slightly raised.

"Why are you keeping me here?" She stood halfway, her voice too loud, too shrill. She realized she crossed a line, but she was frozen in the moment, having inadvertently shattered the quietude of the space.

He scoffed at her expression, his face conveying utter disbelief. "I delivered you from the wilderness." He placed his spoon deliberately into his bowl and leveled a calm gaze at her. "I shared my fire, my food with you." His eyes narrowed and he leaned toward her with a slow, small motion. "I gave you my bed."

Her mouth went dry.

"I helped you find—" He jerked his chin toward the phone. "That. That thing you are so obsessed with." He reached into his lap and withdrew his napkin, folding it into a precise square with slow, deft fingers, never breaking eye contact. "And I am telling you now, that I will not drive these bad back roads on a moonless night, fresh after a torrential storm, on a fifty-mile round trip to the nearest phone." He wiped his mouth. "So, please do tell me what I'm doing *to… you.*" He leaned forward expectantly, his whole body a challenge.

George was startled by the sudden change in his demeanor and faltered. *We're fighting,* she thought, angry with herself. *Why did I start a fight with this man? I gave you my bed,* he'd said, and she was struck with the electric memory of the pine and smoke combined with the less definable scent that was him. A shiver went down her spine as he focused on her intently, his forearms braced on either side of his bowl. She felt as though he was ready to pounce across the table, like a predator. Her breath quickened and she lowered her gaze.

"I'm sorry, that was – not my finest moment." She watched him from the corner of her eye as he relaxed back into his seat. She took a deep breath. "Can I start over?"

"Sure," he replied with just a hint of acid. "I'd love to know more of your fascinating opinions of me." He waited.

She looked down at her hands. She was the asshole. He'd been nothing but kind and accommodating, a complete stranger who didn't owe her a damned thing. She took a deep breath and gave him the summary version, trying not to be emotional or give unnecessary detail. No one wanted to hear a stranger's sad story. She saw his face softening as she explained her family situation, and he murmured sympathetically. She grew more hopeful about salvaging the situation as she continued.

"And, to top it off, the whole reason I was coming up here – to Michigan, I mean, is because I'm supposed to be meeting with a business contact who lives..." She gestured widely. "Somewhere in this vicinity. I was looking for his place when I got lost. I can't get in touch with him to tell him why I'm so late."

Trip looked at her strangely.

"You don't happen to know any of the neighbors around here, do you?" she asked hopefully. "He's been out here for a few months. You may have met him."

"I know all the neighbors from here to town. What business are you in?"

"Music. I work for a label," she answered. "I handle artists."

He grunted softly. "How do you handle them?"

"It's my job to find the source of their motivation so I can keep projects on track. Once I find that, I can get them to do almost anything. I don't manipulate them into doing anything bad," she added quickly on his slight frown. "It's all in their best interest. I keep the train on the tracks. I manage the moving parts so they can focus on making art. The one I'm meeting is having a hard time finishing his album. We're coming up on his release date. So, they sent me to handle him," she finished.

"So, you'll manipulate this sad sack into getting what you need, and then what?"

"I didn't say he was a sad sack," she said with a frown. "He's just a typical creative. After I *motivate* him to wrap up the recording, I go back to LA and get his album finished. Then he becomes someone else's problem."

"Well," he fiddled with his napkin. "Who's this problem you have to handle?"

"Macon. Ben Macon," she said, a question trailing at the end.

His lips tightened and he exhaled through his nose in a huff that seemed like an angry laugh. He shook his head slightly. Did she say something wrong? Had Macon come up here on his bullshit and soured the neighbors after just one summer? *Jesus.*

"He's been expecting me," she added unhelpfully, searching his face.

"All due respect, George, but I don't think he's expecting you."

She cocked her head. "Why do you say that? You *do* know him! Oh, no, what did he—"

"You're looking for Bennett Macon the Third," he interrupted. A small, cynical smile touched his lips. "Or Trip. Whatever pleases you."

Her breath caught as she finally understood. *No. Not possible. Ben Macon was not… this man.* Macon was all hot youth and hard jawline, without a touch of humility in him. He was more handsome than he deserved, a bully, heavy drinker, given to hedonism, an arrogant, self-important, entitled, and did she already say arrogant? Douche.

And then it hit her: that sense of familiarity she'd felt so strongly when she'd first seen him. Those eyes. The height. It *was* him.

My god, he's grown up good, she thought, before she could stop herself.

"You look like you're about to puke."

"I am," she said grimly. She clutched her stomach, consumed with the horror of what was happening.

Ben Macon leaned back and regarded her with a surly expression, then looked away. He suddenly looked exhausted. "Well, this is fun."

8

Mithenness

(n.) The unsettling awareness that the rest of the world happily carries on in your absence; that it is unwilling to wait for you and undergoes massive shifts while your back is turned.

George splashed water on her face in the tiny bathroom off the kitchen and pulled on the same clothes from the day before – the only clothes she had. She was stiff from sleeping on the couch but couldn't bear sleeping in Macon's bed after what he said. Nothing he said would convince her it wasn't going to put him out. The truth was, she wasn't sure she could handle sleeping in the intimacy of his scent again. Some trick of pheromonal attraction tugged at her body when he was close to her. But her brain was just fine, and it sent violent alarm claxons from every synapse. Ben Macon was the enemy, and she walked right into his base and showed her entire hand.

She dug through the cabinets until she found supplies and put on a pot of coffee. *Moment of truth,* she thought, and moved to the table. She reached into the bowl of rice and frowned. She swirled her hand through the slippery grains, but her phone was gone. Macon must have taken it. She wasn't worried about him getting into it because of the bio-metrics, but she wondered why he wanted it.

Last night, after Macon's little reveal, she was so awkward, there had been no way to regain her footing. Every word she uttered was a misstep. She could see it in his eyes. The power dynamic was supposed to land firmly on her side, but it was impossible to summon any sense of dignity now that she'd shoved her foot so firmly in her mouth. All the prattling on about manipulation and handling - she groaned at the thought.

It didn't help knowing Macon had undressed her unconscious body. It was all she could think about. And the cherry on top was her personal past with the man. She had good reason to hate him, so it puzzled her that she gave a single shit about how her words might have affected him. He deserved every iota of her wrath.

She tried shifting the subject to discuss album progress, but he just flicked a sideways glance at her and shut her down.

Not tonight, he said. She figured that was fair, given how her interactions had been with him all day. When he was about to close himself into his bedroom for the night, she blurted out an apology for her behavior, and he told her she shouldn't be so hard on herself. Nothing more. He closed the door behind him, leaving her feeling uncertain and horrid.

She wondered why Macon hadn't brought up Melly the night before. Maybe he genuinely didn't remember George. Even though it was at his second album launch and directly because of George, that he and her best friend had even met in the first place. She was always struck by that cruel little twist of fate – that she, the person who loved Mel the most, was indirectly responsible for her death.

If I hadn't invited her that night, would the trajectory have changed?

Melly and Macon holed up in Nashville soon after that,

and George was still in LA with all her attention on her quickly moving career. She didn't visit much because they were partying hard, and she was newly sober. Not to mention how unpleasantly Macon treated her in those days. Like he was a feral dog, and he'd bite if she came too close.

He *had* been different back then. He was all lean and muscled, the type who pulled off his shirt onstage and went to his knees before the screaming fans. The type to stalk around stage dragging the mic stand behind him with one loose hand in a way that made every hot-blooded human in the room lose their balance. But his transformation was much more than how spectacularly he'd filled out with age. Energetically speaking, he was worlds away from the man she remembered. For one, despite his quiet humor and the subtle moods that shifted across his face, a sense of solitude clung to him. He was like a deep pool of still water. This, alone, was more at odds with her limited memories of him than she could wrap her head around. His manner didn't scream "narcissist." He was mysterious now. Or was he just guarded?

She chewed her lip while she wandered around the living room waiting for the coffee to brew. He wasn't remotely as terrible as he was in her memory. It had been a decade-and-a-half since she last saw him, and time could change people. But that much? Time alone could not redeem what he'd done. She picked up a small stack of worn and dog-eared books underneath the coffee table.

Perfecting Sound Forever.

"Elitist," she said aloud, and dropped the book on the table.

It's So Easy (and other lies).

"Pretentious."

Rip it Up and Start Again.

She smirked. So maybe his taste wasn't bad, but god, if this selection was any indication, he was going to be insufferable. The bottom book on the stack fell to the floor, and she bent to pick it up.

Love is a Mix Tape.

"Unexpectedly sentimental," she muttered. She flipped to a dog-eared section, and a piece of crepey paper fell out. She retrieved it and gently smoothed it open with her fingers. It was a cocktail napkin – just one layer of it, so thin she could see through it. A little pang hit her heart. In Mel's neat, pretty writing with blue ballpoint pen, were lyrics:

> *Yours was the first face that I saw*
> *I think I was blind before I met you*

She thumbed carefully through the book, but nothing else was hidden within. She placed the napkin back into the right spot in between the pages and put the stack back where she'd found it.

Where was he anyway? She moved to the closed green door and put her ear to it. Silence within. She knocked softly.

"Macon?" Nothing.

She walked across the room to the door of the cabin and opened it, and a blast of fresh air tingled her face. She shivered with pleasure and stepped onto the porch, pulling the sweater more closely around her body against the sharp morning breeze.

"Macon!" she called. Her voice echoed over the mist-wreathed water nearby and startled a mallard into flight. He admonished her loudly as he flew up and over the tall ring of pines that enclosed the clearing around the cabin and hugged the far side of the pond. The trees blocked the sun from touching this little pocket just yet. Though the sky was already brightening by degrees, *the fairy ring*, she thought, remained in blue and violet shadow. She turned to check the entrance from the road. Macon's old, green pickup truck was gone.

She moved back into the cabin and approached the green door. She turned the knob as quietly as possible and peeked in.

"Oh!" she murmured, surprised. It was a tiny room, barely office sized, stuffed to the gills with instruments and recording equipment. A ripple of pleasure moved through her: the scent of wood instruments, glue, the slightly acrid smell of new strings, and Macon, himself, filled the little space. She smiled, ran a finger lightly over the knobs of the mixer, carefully stepped over the mic cable and several others snaking along the floor. She twisted her hips strategically as she navigated through the crowded setup. The mass of cables culminated near a sleek silver laptop on a table. She sat down on the battered milk crate in front of it and tapped the space bar. The screen came to life, opening to the desktop. She hesitated, her fingers hovering over the keyboard.

I really shouldn't, she thought, and then pulled up a finder window and searched for "final mix." Immediately a string of files showed up, and she clicked on one of the audio tracks. She picked up the cans that snaked from the computer and settled them over her ears, descending into total silence. She clicked play.

Acoustic guitar came in first for a measure, then some

subtle banjo, way back in mix. She closed her eyes and settled into the melody. Stand-up bass rounded out the bottom. Lead acoustic came in, gentle picking that floated over the rhythm. She always wondered how he played such delicate things with such big hands. Macon's rich, slightly rough baritone flooded her ears. Tender and sad, his voice tore a small avalanche of emotion from her chest. The wordplay was genius.

She finished, savoring it until the last sustaining note faded to silence and the track stopped. She pulled off the headphones and set them on the table with a dazed expression. She didn't remember his music having this much depth. There was no doubt about it. The song would be a hit when it was finished.

She looked at the list of files still waiting in the finder window.

A bird warbled outside. The sun just started to crest the tops of the tall trees. She closed all of the file folders and carefully shut the laptop, trying to make sure everything looked like it did when she entered the room. She moved quickly to leave as she felt a rush of guilt. She shouldn't have gone into his computer. She realized she would have to pretend she didn't know about this music, even though his song already had its hooks in her. She wanted to listen to it again; to absorb it with her body and let it wring all the sorrow out of her wounded heart. To soften her enough that maybe she'd be able to really cry.

Outside, the rumble of his approaching truck startled her into action, and she sprung to close the recording room door quickly. She ran to the table and sat down quickly, cupping her coffee and forcing herself to breathe slowly and relax. She carefully wiped her face of any telltale looks. The truck door slammed, and the crunch of boots on gravel approached. Macon whistled a little tune as he walked. His heavy footsteps sounded on the deck. He threw open the door and appeared in the doorway, larger than life. He eyed her as he came in with a little gust of fresh air that pushed a leaf along the floor.

"Hey," he said.

"Hey," she replied breathlessly.

He frowned. "What's uh… what's goin' on?"

"Just having some coffee," she said, and gestured around the room. "Doing… morning stuff."

He looked around doubtfully. "Okay. I'd say you're being weird, but maybe this is just the way you are." He reached into the inside breast pocket of his coat and withdrew a small, flat package wrapped in a brown paper bag. "Here." He plunked it down on the table before her. "Don't say I never did anything for you," he added gruffly.

She picked it up and unwrapped it, revealing her phone, beautifully intact. She looked up quizzically.

"It only took two days to forget how to turn it on?" he teased.

She fumbled with the little button and screamed when it powered up. He watched her with a mixture of amusement and mystification. She stood so quickly her chair tipped and clattered to the ground.

"Thank you, thank you." George melted with relief. She placed her hand over her heart. "You've saved me."

"It wasn't *that* big of a deal." He shifted uncomfortably. "You'll want to go up in the loft to get the best signal."

She could cry, she was so happy. In fact, a lump did rise

up in her throat. "*Thank you*," she said again, emphatically. "However you managed this, and why…" she trailed off. He stood up a little straighter under her approval, clearly pleased at her reaction. A little of the wariness between them seemed to fade.

Ding. They both looked at the phone in her hand with surprise, like they'd forgotten it existed. *Ding. Ding dingdingding.*

"Uh oh, here we go," she said, and grimaced.

He wrinkled his nose. "I'm going to work on some mixes and let you… *handle*," he said pointedly, "whoever it is who needs motivation today." She tried to wither him with her look, but he was too busy eyeing her phone with distaste as the deluge of notifications poured in. "I can't believe you're so excited to have that thing working again."

"I may rescind my earlier gratitude," she said wryly as she watched the number of notifications rise over her text and inbox icons. She threw him a distracted, apologetic smile, and turned off the volume. "I'll try to be quiet."

He nodded and retreated into the recording room with one dark look back at her, shut the door behind him, and left her to deal with the mess that awaited.

She looked down at her phone and said, "Hey Siri, call…" then paused. *Kato or Lucia or Aunt Carla?* Siri undulated patiently. "Call Lucia." She felt as though some larger decision had just been made, but she wasn't sure exactly what it was. A queasy feeling rolled over her.

"Darling!" Lucia's voice on the other end of the line crackled, the tenuous connection barely holding.

The halting and somewhat confusing conversation that followed was nothing short of a disaster. It seemed that, in the short time she'd been out of commission, Misha, one of the interns she managed, had been assigned to be the label rep at the Yung Karl launch party. She and the young rapper hit it off to the point his manager had called Lucia directly to encourage Misha's deeper involvement in his team. He liked her fresh ideas. *Ugh.* George was fairly devastated to learn the beautiful twenty-two-year-old – whom she'd *handpicked* – had seized the very first moment to fuck her over. George didn't care what kind of fresh ideas she had, that *child* wasn't ready to stand in George's shoes. A wash of disbelief, then panic, then anger eventually faded into numbness as she sat, staring at her dark phone.

Her entire being told her to fly back to LA and nip this situation in the bud immediately, do damage control, reassert her strength – but she couldn't possibly.

Aunt Carla. The boys. Macon. Shit. She scrolled to her recents and dialed Aunt Carla's landline. George let it ring for several minutes before she hung up and texted her aunt's mobile.

> *Had an accident, was out of commission.*
> *Totally fine now, sorry I was MIA*
> *Call me when you can xx*

George watched for a response, but there was no indication of whether or not her message was received.

She called Kato and he picked up immediately, but it turned out he hadn't been worried about her at all. He just assumed she was working, that Macon's cabin in the woods was off grid. He frustrated her further by not being upset at all by her misadventure, given that everything had turned out in her favor. He told her to give Macon his gratitude, which made her want to strangle him. He then had the audacity to tell her he was sure Misha wasn't being malicious, and that everything would be straightened out when she got back.

As if this was supposed to be comforting somehow, reminding her that she'd be languishing away from home for three more weeks. She gritted her teeth. Why couldn't he just be angry on her behalf? Why did he have to meet all the hardness of life with such complete steadiness and reason? She hated it sometimes. She wondered what was wrong with her that she desired his anger, his need, his fight, the worst in him. That she wanted to diminish him somehow for her own gratification, to appease her own pain. But she couldn't rationalize herself out of feeling stung and lonely, and that made her feel even worse about herself. At this rate, she'd be punishing herself all day. She sighed. Maybe it was just being back in a place she worked so hard to escape that was making her feel so… self-pitying.

She stood and walked to the front door, opened it and stepped out onto the deck. The sun was directly overhead, the sky, a cloudless expanse of washed-out blue. Clear light filled the fairy ring, glinting off the surface of the pond and its border of browning reeds.

The world was still spinning, and everyone was living their lives. She disappeared for almost three days, and not only did the world not stop, but the only person who knew or cared about the danger she'd been in was the last man on earth she wanted to have any level of relationship with.

Macon was at least partially responsible for Mel's death. And she was stuck here with him in this time dilation bubble, where nothing moved except for the sun across the sky, and the pond would go on forever sparkling in the fall light, while everyone and everything else was forging forward at a thousand miles per hour without her.

My life couldn't be more fucked, she thought, and immediately wished she hadn't dared think it at all.

At some point that afternoon, frowning in concentration as she chipped away at her email, hunched over her phone on a storage box in the loft, Macon slipped out. She barely registered the front door shutting behind him, but in the periphery of her conscious brain, she noticed when the engine of his truck roared to life, then the sound of its retreat down the drive.

She finally looked up, took off her glasses, and rubbed the bridge of her nose. She was glad he hadn't acknowledged her; she needed some space to get her head straight.

She looked at the text thread with her aunt once more and added three little hearts after her last message. Still nothing.

9

Grayshift

(n.) The tendency for goals and benchmarks to feel huge
when viewed in advance, only to fade into banality as
soon as you've achieved them—finally reaching the top
of the ladder, only to notice it circling back around like a
hamster wheel.

George pulled into the drive, past the willow trees and
up to the front of the farmhouse. She turned the key in
the ignition and paused for a moment before unlatching her
seat belt and opening the car door. Aunt Carla's old Honda
was still in the driveway. George unloaded the trunk, expecting at any moment for the front door to fly open, to see her
aunt's familiar form, Sandy bounding out past her ankles.
But all was quiet.

She tried the front door and found it locked. Aunt Carla
never locked her doors. She put down her bags and pushed
her face against the window, cupping her hands around her
eyes. George frowned and hopped off the porch, stamping
down the unmown grass as she skirted around the side of the
house to the back. She tried the sliding door and groaned
with relief when it moved fluidly on its tracks. She let herself
in and retrieved her bags from the front, then moved from
room to room calling for her aunt. The house was still and
quiet, with an energy about it that it hadn't been inhabited

for a time. A growing feeling of dread tingled at the back of her neck.

She checked her phone. Still no response on text. She tried Aunt Carla's cell and heard a faint ringing from another part of the house. She followed the chiming sounds until the voicemail picked up, then called again, repeating the exercise until she found herself at the bathroom door, off her aunt's main bedroom. She tried to swallow and found her tongue dry as a board. She slowly pushed open the door, bracing for whatever she might find, but the bathroom was empty and clean. She frowned. The ringtone echoed against the 360 tile surfaces, bouncing the sound around the small room, but George finally zeroed in on it, wedged on the floor behind the toilet. *What the hell?*

She bent to pick it up and the home screen slid into view. There were twenty-seven notifications. She opened and scrolled through her aunt's texts, dating back to two afternoons ago. She looked around, searching for any sign of where her aunt and the kids might have gone, and came up empty-handed. She searched the messy face of the fridge, covered with children's art, receipts, pizza delivery coupons, and themed magnets from every state. She fell into a chair and slumped. Maybe they were just out doing something.

She just needed to be patient and wait.

She hated waiting.

Georgia was wrapped up in a virtual meeting when the phone on the wall jangled. She jumped at the loud intrusion and found herself halfway across the room before she even realized she wasn't sitting anymore. She snatched the phone from the wall-mounted receiver.

"Hello?"

"Is this Georgia?" an unfamiliar woman's voice on the other end of the line.

"Yes," George's heart was pounding so hard she could barely speak.

"Hi Georgia, I'm Nelly from Wilkin's Hospice Center. Your aunt is in the hospital, and they're about to move her here."

"What happened?" Georgia exhaled. Thank god it wasn't the police notifying next-of-kin.

"I'm not sure about the details," Nelly said apologetically. George didn't respond.

"We were told we could reach you here. I've been calling for two days," she explained. "I'm sorry to bear bad news." She allowed an appropriate amount of breathing room before she continued crisply. "I'd like to give you the list of things your aunt has requested you bring by. She'll be here by 4PM today."

George finished the call and looked down at the list. *Fuzzy socks, pink robe, nightgown, Snoopy shirt, craft box, green journal, toothbrush, shampoo, heating pad, comfrey balm.* She added a few items of her own at the end, then checked her laptop, but the virtual meeting had ended.

She moved around Aunt Carla's room, gathering her things, and felt a flush of guilt at all the photos of herself next to pictures of dad, Henry, Hannah, and the mess of kids between them. Henry, in the last years of his short life, seemed hell-bent on procreating with as many women as he could. The result was six additional children scattered across central Indiana. Aunt Carla didn't love the situation but met it with good humor. She was over the moon to have so many grandchildren and took copious photos of them.

George hardly visited after her dad died, and never after Grandma passed. But Aunt Carla had built a veritable shrine to George. Not just the photos of their visits, but pictures she pulled off social media, of George at launch parties and fancy soirees. She picked up a framed picture of herself with Kato at a red-carpet affair. She wore a floor-length, sparkling ball gown with a low-cut neckline that highlighted her best features, and Kato looked like a star in a tailored designer suit that fit all his long, muscular lines just right. They were fighting that night. Despite their convincing smiles and movie star looks, she could see the tension in their arms as they held themselves slightly away from one another. The memory made her frown.

She browsed through the other photos of herself. Though she was smiling in all of them, she remembered how stressed out she'd been at every single one of those events. When she stopped drinking, it became easier in some ways. Easier to handle the stress, to keep her head clear. But harder because there wasn't anything left to soften what was left over after the momentary thrill of a successful launch. None of these captured moments involved joyful memories, beyond the satisfaction she felt when she was able to tick off a box next to a goal she achieved. Interspersed in the pictures were a slew of family moments she wasn't present for. She realized she didn't even know the boys' birthdays. Surly and out of sorts and feeling badly about herself, she packed up the rest of the items in a hurry and bolted from the house. The ghosts of her past followed on her heels, nipping, casting doubt, drawing slow blood as she ran to her car.

Forty-five minutes later, George rolled down her windows and pulled out of a CVS parking lot and onto the State Highway. The plastic bag on the seat next to her fluttered around the sudoku, crossword books, and other goodies she picked up for Aunt Carla. She called Kato as she waited at a red light, and his voice sprang up on the car stereo. He sounded out of breath and she said so.

"I just ran up from the garage. You won't guess who I was just talking to…"

"Weird Mary?" she guessed, and he laughed.

"Weird Mary moved months ago – no, Adam came by," he said.

"And…?"

"I have a project."

She waited for a few moments for him to elaborate. "Great!" she answered, wondering why he was being so cagey.

"In Sweden," said Kato, and she could tell by the way he said it that he was grimacing on the other end of the line.

"Wow! That's exciting."

"It's an outdoor collab with Goulden Renfrew and transluna," he continued excitedly.

"Transluna… why do I know that name–" she searched.

"The non-binary Mexican artist who does the moving water and light installations—"

"Right! This is incredible. Congratulations!" She beamed as she drove. Goulden was a well-established artist, and transluna, an up-and-coming genius designer. This was likely to be a career-maker for Kato, vaulting him into the next level of his professional journey. A thrill ran through her on his behalf. "What piece are you doing?"

"I'm modifying the *Spirits of Things* concept to work with the pieces the other two will be building with me. We've only had one virtual preliminary meeting, but we're all really vibing on concept."

"Holy shit, babe. This is massive." She was genuinely excited. "What's your timeline?"

"Ah, yeah. That's the thing. They want us in Stockholm Monday," he said, and she thought she detected a forced nonchalance. "We'll be working on this for the next six months." She heard him breathe in and hold it.

A million thoughts crowded her head.

I *need you here, what about Aunt Carla's funeral, how can I possibly manage life without you there, have you arranged a cat sitter, are you worried about being away that long, are you worried about me…*

But she thought of him holding his breath back in LA. Like he was afraid she would deny him this opportunity, and she hated that. So, she just said, "Babe, I really couldn't be happier for you. Go. You have to."

He exhaled on the other end, and she knew he felt better.

Whatever came next, she would work it out on her own.

Aunt Carla was in bright spirits when George walked into the small, cheery room in the hospice facility, an old Victorian house in the center of the city. George could see the Capitol building from the window, and below there was a rose garden in a small fenced front courtyard, now colorful with rose hips and red leaves. She draped the fuzzy blanket on her aunt's frail body and together they went through the bags of goodies.

"Aunt Carla, where are the boys?" George asked, as her aunt happily fingered a roll of ribbon from the craft box.

"I'm going to make little scrapbooks for all my grandba-bies," she said cheerfully. George's eyes narrowed.

"Are you on morphine?"

"Yes," answered Aunt Carla with a smile.

George sighed. "Shit." She pulled a chair from the corner and dragged it next to the bed. "Aunt Carla," George touched her wrist lightly. Aunt Carla looked up at her with unfocused eyes.

"Aunt Carla, where are the boys?"

Aunt Carla frowned and put one finger against her lip. It would have been comical in any other situation, but George was starting to worry.

"Do you know where Michael and Jack are right now?"

Her aunt looked up, gaining a moment of lucidity. "Barbara and Kent have them. They're safe." She nodded once to signal she was done saying what she had to say.

Who the fuck are Barbara and Kent?

"How do I get in touch with them?" George leaned in and tapped her aunt's wrist again, as her attention had already drifted back to the bag of treats.

"Help me put these socks on," Carla said, and held up the Snoopy shirt. George admitted defeat, pulled the fuzzy socks from the bag, and carefully fitted them on her aunt's wrinkled little feet. She rubbed the balls of her thumbs across Aunt Carla's arches and heels, and the woman sighed in contentment and leaned back against the pillow. She was almost asleep by the time George finished. George put away all the items she brought and left the puzzle books and pencils near the bed with a note.

On the way out she gave the staff all her information and

they promised to get in touch with her as soon as her aunt woke up in the morning, before they gave her any more morphine. The head nurse was a solid woman with a calming, motherly air about her. When she explained the medical particulars of what was happening, her manner kept George from panicking.

Two weeks, maybe three, said the nurse. *Depends on whether or not she'll eat. Time will tell, but she is nearing the end of this journey.* The woman told her kindly that the best way she could serve her aunt would be to go home and get some rest so she could function.

Now she sat at the kitchen table, the single overhead fixture making a weak circle of light in the otherwise dark and empty house. It was 1AM and there was nothing she could do for anyone. Her mind was racing, her adrenaline up from the unexpected events of the day.

George found chamomile in the gallon bag full of random tea bags and made herself a cup of tea. *God, I'm never going to get to sleep,* she thought miserably, and rubbed the bridge of her nose, in her characteristic manner.

10

Natsukashii

(adj.) A warm sadness when a memory hits you so gently
it hurts.

George squinted and smacked her dry lips. She ran her knuckles over her eyes, against the sun that shone through the little north-facing kitchen window. Its rays threw thousands of rainbows from her aunt's suncatcher collection across the floor and walls, and over the tabletop where she'd fallen asleep. She groaned and sat up stiffly, looked at the wall clock. She slept for eight straight hours and her back remembered every minute of it.

She reached for her laptop before she realized it was Saturday. She'd been here just over a week, and everything was still a mess. Significantly worse, even.

She threw back the leftover cold chamomile tea, swishing it around until her tongue no longer felt like a rug in her mouth.

She walked into her aunt's room and fell back onto the thick quilt. She lay there for a while, watching the light move across the ceiling. There was an almost tangible sense of peace in the room. She breathed in and out slowly. Muscles in her neck and back began to release and she sunk into the bed, a warm sunbeam falling across her belly. The light shifted gently and her mind settled. Calm settled over her, and eventually, she drifted off to sleep.

George thanked the head nurse and turned away, looking at the number on the little slip of paper. She walked outside, into the early afternoon sun and tapped the number into her phone. It rang once before a raspy voice picked up.

"Hi, this is Georgia Robinson, I'm Carla Williams' niece. I heard you've been taking care of Jack and Michael."

"Oh, hi Georgia, I've heard a lot about you – from Hannah. And from Carla, of course. We're out here in Franklin, but we're here if you need anything. We could bring the boys by tomorrow if you want, after church." Georgia was all too grateful to have some extra space while she worked out all the things that needed to happen next. But there was something cautious, defensive, almost, about the woman's manner.

"Thank you, Barbara. I'm looking forward to meeting y'all." They said goodbyes and hung up. She couldn't identify where the tension came from between Barbara and herself, and it left her with a feeling of trepidation.

George walked through the hospice house with a light step, trying to be respectful of the patients at rest in the rooms leading off the long hallway. She frowned as she neared her aunt's room. Muffled cackling and hoots came from behind the door. She threw it open, and four, strange, expectant faces smiled up at her.

"My coven has arrived," Aunt Carla crowed, and they all grinned. George ran her eyes over the disparate group. One woman, tall and willowy with wild, faded red hair that fell to her back, wore sandals and jeans with a bright-orange, fluttering peasant blouse. A petite woman with a perfectly turned-out bob stood by the edge of the bed, clasping her aunt's hand. She was a relic from another time in a conservative pinafore style dress in muted grays, and an impossibly straight posture. The other wore bright pink lipstick and matching '80s shades hooked on her neckline, her bosom straining a sweater featuring a pink kitten in the middle. On the chair by the bed sat a brown-haired woman with rosy cheeks and wire-rimmed glasses, clutching a box full of lemon squares. She looked closer to George's age than the rest of the women, who were all in their late sixties. She smiled up at George as Aunt Carla made introductions. Something about her face made George want to hug her.

"Okay, okay, let's get back to it," said Deena, the redhead from North Carolina. "George, we were just talking about setting up the altar in here, and what the best place to do that would be. I think it should be on the table, and we should move the table into the corner."

Little Helen, the small woman in the old-fashioned gray dress, flew in from Cleveland where she lived with her husband, both pastors at the local church. Deb, kitten sweater, was a published poet and lived nearby. Tanya, the younger woman, was a friend from Al-Anon.

Together, they rearranged all the furniture around in the small room until everything was set up to their satisfaction. The altar sat neatly on a beaded cloth on the table, full of interesting rocks and feathers, and pictures of all the grandkids. And of course, Hannah and Henry.

Little Helen sat at Carla's bedside, softly talking about what kind of service Carla wanted, and speaking frankly about death in her soothing way, as the other women decorated the room.

Deb hung a string of twinkle lights around the window. George rearranged all the cut flowers and tucked them around the room. Tanya set up Carla's bedside table so everything she would want was within easy reach.

They all stood back and admired their work. Carla beamed. They spent the rest of the afternoon telling animated stories as her aunt wheezed with hysterical laughter. George sat back and soaked it all in. Most of the friendships spanned decades. Fifty years, for Deb. They told wild stories about the adventures they shared – hitchhiking across the country in the 70s; epic, cocaine-fueled parties in the 80s; legendary overseas girls' trips in the 90s, and by the early 2000s, more than a handful of divorces between them. George loved hearing the lore behind the other half of her aunt's life. They hung out for hours, and George felt like she had three new aunties and a cousin by the time she left.

Welzschmerz

(n.) A deep, painful sadness caused by comparing the imperfect world to the world you wished existed.

The drive back to Michigan was pensive. George didn't particularly want to leave when the clock was ticking down on Aunt Carla's life, but she needed to get Macon on track, and Carla's coven would be in town to keep her company for the duration. She felt most useful doing something productive, and that meant work.

Kato was leaving today for Sweden. She tried to have feelings about it. To think about the ramifications of his absence. But all she felt was a numb pit in her belly.

After meeting with Barbara, it seemed there would be some competition for the boys. The woman was dead set on keeping them, and George didn't really know how she felt about that. They already knew Barbara. The boys were comfortable with her. She was familiar. She was *local*. George drove with the car stereo off, lost in thought the whole way. She heaved a sigh of relief as she turned off the highway onto the driveway to Macon's house. It was a warm day for this time of year, and she approached the fairy ring slowly, inhaling the warm pine scent of the forest around her.

As her car rumbled to a stop on the bumpy rock driveway, movement at the corner of her eye caught her attention.

She turned the key and sat in silence, then leaned forward to peer through the windshield.

"Jesus Christ," she muttered. Macon stood across the wide lawn with his back partially toward her, his red flannel and white t-shirt thrown over the branch of a nearby tree. His torso was bare, and what a torso it was. *Ye Gods*, she thought, *this man's back is causing me to have a religious experience right now.* She stared as he bent to pick up a sizeable billet and placed it on the block, then swung his axe and split the thick piece of wood in two with a single stroke. The thick muscles of his back and those under his heavily inked sleeves rippled in the soft sunlight. George fanned her face. The sun was *really* beating down. Suddenly Macon turned and looked in her direction. He caught her eyes through the windshield, lifted his chin, and waved before turning back to the wood pile.

George blushed. "Goddammit," she muttered. She unloaded the car and got everything inside. There was a folded piece of paper on the coffee table with her name written in fat black letters. She plucked it up and opened it.

"Look upstairs," she read aloud, and looked around. "Guess he means the loft." She tossed the note down on the table and climbed the ladder to the small loft space. The bright smell of freshly cut pine blasted her as her head rose over the threshold. There was a small platform bedframe made of untreated pine. It was still so pale and fragrant, it must have been newly made. Same for the little side table. A water glass sat atop its smoothly sanded top held a small bundle of dried flowers. There was another piece of paper on the bed that said, "You can stay up here when you're around. – M"

She dropped the note back onto the bed, a twin mattress

topped with a pretty, vintage-looking quilt and a single pillow. He even ran an extension cord up from downstairs and secured it to the wall next to her nightstand so she could plug in her phone. She looked around and gaped in disbelief. He'd done this for *her*? Last time she was here, there was just a clothesline and some boxes up here. She shook her head slightly. She didn't understand how this could be the same person she once knew, and it was fucking with her head. She was having all kinds of unwelcome feelings about someone *she knew, factually,* was a villain, and she wanted to smack herself. Sometimes she just didn't understand what was wrong with her brain. Why would her body go all askew around him when her head was too well aware that he could be a genuine danger to her? The things Mel told her… it felt simply impossible to reconcile that with this. But she'd have to. George couldn't afford to let him lull her into a false sense of security.

Macon returned to the cabin a few hours later, his clothing thankfully restored, with an armful of firewood. George stood at the tiny kitchen counter, trying to transform the groceries she brought into a meal.

"Dammit," she muttered, as the dull kitchen knife smashed a tomato she was trying to slice. Macon stood from where he was watching the freshly kindled fire grow in the stove and stepped into the kitchen. He caught George's wrist as she moved in to torture another vegetable and peeled the knife out of her fingers wordlessly as she gaped at him.

"What're you…" she murmured.

"Just gimme a minute, here." He gently pushed her aside to reach into the drawer and pulled out a whetstone. He spent a few moments moving the blade over its surface with skilled hands, then wiped the knife on a towel and flipped it around in his hand so the handle was extended toward her.

She looked down at it for a few moments, then took it and turned to the food, and breathed a sigh of relief as it sliced cleanly through the tomato. "Thank you, Macon."

"No problem." He hovered and watched her deftly and quickly work her way through the remaining vegetables. "What're you making?"

"Shakshuka. That work for you?"

"I have no idea what it is, but I'm sure it'll be better than canned chili. Do you need help?"

"No, I'd go nuts if you tried to help me in this space. By the way…" She paused and leaned back against the counter to face him. "Thanks for setting up a spot for me in the loft. I really appreciate that."

He nodded slightly. "Figured you'd be in and out a couple times over the next few weeks. There's nowhere else to stay around here."

"I appreciate that, too. Also, I uh… I want to apologize for what I said on the first night I was here. I've felt really shitty about it. I'm just here to help, Makes." She slipped and used Melly's nickname for him. She looked up, startled. But he didn't seem to notice and continued staring at a spot on the wall across the room with a faraway look in his eyes.

"You already apologized, remember? It's fine," he finally said. "I know I'm past schedule."

"So, can we talk business?" she asked hopefully. "I just want to know where we are."

"After dinner," he answered. "I'm too hungry to talk about it now. And I don't discuss business while I'm eating."

"Fancy policy for a man who lives on canned stew."

He laughed suddenly, resonant and deep, and the sound filled up the cabin. "Hey, I'm only eating like this because I haven't had time to hunt or get the garden harvested yet."

She turned back to the food and continued working. "Garden? You've only been here for eight weeks."

"I live here." He leaned against the wall and hooked a thumb into his belt loop as he watched her cook.

She turned on the gas under the cast iron skillet before she turned to face him again. "This is a vacation rental."

"That's a fact."

"The label is paying for a vacation rental."

He nodded. "You're on a roll, Peaches."

She stiffened at his use of her old nickname. So, he *did* know who she was. Weird that he hadn't said anything. She supposed she hadn't either, so, who was really the weird one?

"But... I thought you lived in Nashville?"

"I did. Label still sends checks there because my management firm is there."

"But what do you even do out here? How are you playing shows?"

"I left pretty much right after Mel... When I tour, I'm on tour. When I'm home, I'm here. Don't care much for crowds these days."

She sat down heavily in one of the chairs, and he followed her. He braced his forearms on the table and their eyes locked.

"You knew who I was? This whole time?"

He snorted and his eyebrows came together in a look that suggested both irritation and confusion. "Georgia, come on. What in the fuck kind of question is that? How could you think I'd forget you? Fuck." He swiped a hand across his face. "I almost find that offensive. No, I do. I find it offensive, alright?"

"I just thought…" She stopped talking and shook her head. She looked away, then got up and checked the skillet, keeping her back to him. "I'm sorry, Makes. But why didn't you say something?"

"Why didn't you, George?"

"Fair question." She moved the vegetables around in the pan as they finally started to soften into a sauce. "I legitimately didn't recognize you with that beard. And then when you told me, I was so embarrassed I didn't know what to say. But you knew from the start."

"I didn't," he admitted. "Not quite. I knew the second you stepped out of my bedroom in the full light of day, though. Sorry I didn't say anything, but I figured maybe you just didn't want to talk about it." His eyes fell to his fingers, where he toyed with a fork. "I can understand if that wound is too sore to touch."

George didn't know how to respond, so she turned away and grabbed the eggs out of the fridge. She carefully cracked them into the depressions she made in the sauce. He watched her for a few seconds.

"You know, I need to tell you, all that stuff Mel said about what was going on with us…"

"Macon."

He stopped talking.

"I can't talk about this. Not with you."

"Let me say this one thing, okay? I need to tell you this. I want the air to be clear between us… so we can work together."

She sighed as she covered the skillet and took her seat

again. "Fine. Get it out. I don't know if this is a good idea, though."

"I never touched her, George. I would *never* have hurt her."

"She emailed me photos of your fingerprints bruised onto her arms." George spat. She didn't intend to speak, but she couldn't let that one go. Her jaw tightened as she tried to control her breathing.

He met her eyes and held them. "November 27, 2008. Thanksgiving Day. She came after me with a cast iron skillet. Managed to wallop me pretty good before I wrestled it away from her." He turned in his chair and parted his thick, silver and black hair. He ran one finger over a fat, white scar. "Thirty stitches. As soon as I got the pan away from her, she made a dash for the knife block. I had to subdue her while I called the cops. I was worried she'd seriously hurt me or herself. I just held her down. I was bleeding like crazy, and it got all over her. When the cops got there, they arrested me and I spent the night in jail puking from the concussion."

She looked away uncomfortably and tried to stifle the feelings of hurt and rage that rose in her chest. "Macon, I don't…"

"Please hear me, Georgia. I *didn't*. I didn't hurt her, I didn't hit her, I didn't cheat, none of it. She was so fucking mad at me when I started trying to get sober. She told a lot of people a lot of things. The worst thing I ever did to her," he began. He stopped and took a deep breath. "Worst thing I ever did to her was that I stayed. I stayed and kept getting her out of trouble. She wasn't ready to get clean, and I kept slipping back in. I could always stop, but I couldn't stay. She just… she had shit hidden all over the house."

George didn't know what to say. Didn't know what was

true. She stood and checked the eggs, then occupied herself for the next several minutes serving up the contents of the skillet. She put a bowl in front of Macon, then sat down and stared into her dish. She finally looked up at him and found his gaze meeting hers.

"It's just hard to believe none of it was your doing. I *do* remember how you treated me, for one. You were such an asshole," she said quietly. "You acted like you didn't want me around. Worse than that. You were so hostile."

"Yeah. Because she got so bad every time you left," he agreed. "I *didn't* want you around. You'd leave and she'd start questioning why you were so successful and she was such a mess, and it would turn into a manic episode, and that would turn into going all the way off the rails. Every *fucking* time, Georgia. I was so scared of what would happen in your wake. And tired. I was so damn tired. You were the harbinger of another relapse. For both of us."

A cold chill ran down George's spine at the revelation. She speared a piece of egg on her fork and dipped it in the bright red sauce. She forced herself to eat despite her sour stomach. She didn't know what to think anymore. She wondered if Mel could have been lying to her the whole time for the reasons Macon gave her. She reluctantly concluded it was not only plausible, but it was the most probable version of the story. Mel reminded her a lot of her cousin, Hannah. But brighter, burning hotter all the time. A wild sparkle of beauty and charisma that commanded rooms when she was good. A black ball of self-loathing that lashed out with razor claws when she was low. Her lips felt numb.

"I don't know if this is a good or bad time to change the subject, but this is delicious, George. Thanks for cooking."

She pushed her bowl away, still half-full. She didn't want to talk about Mel anymore, and the smell of the food was making her feel sick. There was nowhere to hide in the tiny cabin, so she did the next best thing and simply changed the subject. "Let's talk about the album."

"I told you. Not until we're done eating." He eyed her as he slowly lifted a fork full of peppers and egg to his mouth and chewed.

"Oh, my god." She rolled her eyes and stood. She turned around with her bowl in hand and started cleaning up the kitchen. She didn't have the wherewithal to deal with Macon's bullshit after a conversation like that. Her mind was still reeling.

She'd been manipulated by her dead best friend into misjudging someone so profoundly that she needlessly carried the burning toxicity of it for years. Probably. It was a lot to take in. Maybe even harder than what was happening with her family right now. And it wasn't the first time she'd heard from someone else that Mel had lied to her, near the end. Once she started to accept it, all the confusing, little pieces that never seemed to fit into the narrative she'd been holding clicked into place like a finished puzzle. The truth that confronted her was blinding and unsettling.

She was still absently running the sponge around the inside of the bowl when she was startled from her thoughts. Macon bumped her hip with his and pushed her out of the way.

"Please, go chill, George. I'll clean all this up. I'm really sorry. I know I just dumped a lot on you, but I've been wanting to tell you this for a lot of years. I feel better, even if you don't believe me."

She put her bowl in the small wire dish drainer without a word and retreated to the little loft just above the kitchen.

12

Harke

(n.) A painful memory that you look back upon with unexpected fondness, even though you remember having dreaded it at the time; a tough experience that has since been overridden by the pride of having endured it, the ca- maraderie of those you shared it with, or the satisfaction of having a good story to tell.

George had barely settled in when her phone buzzed. She pulled it from the charger and answered. "This is George," she said. After a few seconds of silence, her eyes widened and a little cry escaped her throat. "Thank you," she finally said. "I'll be there as soon as possible."

She threw the phone on the floor and leaned over her knees, sucking in deep breaths to stop the panic attack that was already starting to tighten her chest.

Macon looked up and turned off the water. "What's going on?" He waited and dried off his hands, then pulled himself up the ladder until he could see over the edge of the loft floor. "Whoa. Hey, what's up?"

"That was the nursing home. Aunt Carla died." She breathed in and out evenly. *Don't pass out.* "I thought I had two weeks," she said numbly. "I have to go."

She stood on unsteady legs and started to move toward the ladder. Macon hopped off to let her pass and watched as she gathered her things. "George."

She was too focused on making a "next steps" list on her phone to hear him.

"Georgia."

She looked up. "What?"

"I can't let you leave. It's already dark. Storm's blowing through tonight. You're in no condition to be making that drive."

She stared at him. "I have to go back. My aunt is dead. I said I'd be there…"

He cut her off. "She's still gonna be gone in the morning. No one's doing anything tonight whether you're there or not." He gave her a little push toward the couch. "Sit down with me. I'll make coffee."

She shook her head vehemently and surged toward her keys. "I'm fine, I really am." Macon stepped forward ahead of her and neatly plucked them away before she could pick them up. He pulled off the car key and tucked it in his back pocket.

"Macon! I'm fine!" She was wild-eyed and breathing heavily. Macon thought she might imminently faint.

"Georgia. Sit. Down." The authoritative tone and volume of his command broke through her haze, and she sat down in the center of the couch.

She let her breath out in a rush. "Fuck," she said in a small voice. "I need to call Kato."

"What time is it in Sweden?"

She wailed in despair as she looked at her world clock. "It's only 3:30 in the morning there!"

"Great. Listen, I'm not letting you leave tonight. I'm sorry. But as a friend, a concerned citizen, a professional acquaintance – no. You're not in great shape. It's not safe for you to be on the road." He grabbed her arm and held it out, so she'd have to acknowledge how badly her hands were trembling.

She fell back against the cushions and groaned.

"What time does Kato wake up? We'll sit up, have some coffee, talk about what you need before you leave tomorrow. In a couple hours, you can call him. Go to bed. Wake up early and get on the road."

It did make sense. But she felt like she'd burst, twiddling her thumbs for hours in the confines of the cabin. She told him as much.

"How much time do we need to burn?"

She looked at her phone again. "Ugh. Four hours."

"I have an idea, hold on. Coffee's almost done." He stood and moved to an upper cabinet, from which he extracted a large green thermos. He watched patiently as the coffee finished brewing before he poured the whole pot in. He turned. "How'd you like it?"

"Cream, a little sugar."

He finished mixing it and moved back to the couch. He extended his hand. "Get up, we're going out."

"I thought it was supposed to rain?" She took his hand and he hauled her out of the squishy cushions.

"Put on your shoes, Georgia."

She wasn't accustomed to being ordered around. She wasn't sure she would have been cool with it under normal circumstances, but it was a relief to relinquish control at the moment. She pulled on her boots and the coat Macon handed her, and followed him outside.

They crunched across the rocks until they were in the soft, dewy grass. Moonlight glinted off the pond, and they trailed thin clouds of breath as they walked. Macon led her to the edge of the water. The back end of a rowboat pulled halfway up into the mud bobbed on the surface of the water. He unraveled the mooring rope from the stump where it was tied and motioned for George to get in.

"Are you serious? Right now, in the dark?" She frowned down at the boat.

"It's safe enough, we're only going a little way."

She looked around the pond with a dubious expression. "I'd say so. Can't be more than sixty feet to the other side."

"Get in, George." He pointed at the bench seat.

She heaved a sigh and carefully got into the boat, grateful it was still stuck into the shore. Macon pushed it into the water and hopped in lightly before settling on the bench and picking up an oar. He handed her the thermos.

"Drink that."

"Jeez, bossy," George muttered, but she obediently unscrewed the cap and took a sip. "That's nice," she murmured.

Macon pushed the oar through the water and soon they were floating in the center of the pond. He kept rowing until they were gliding straight toward the wall of cattails at the far side. Georgia raised her hands defensively and squeaked as they headed straight for the shore. She squeezed her eyes shut for the moment of impact she anticipated. But none came, and seconds later, they were still moving forward. The rattling and soft scrape of dry grass on the side of the boat filled her ears. She cracked her eyes to find Macon looking back at her, a little smile curving his lips.

"It's a tiny inlet. It connects to the lake," he explained, then turned to look ahead again as he continued to push them forward. "The pond is really my own little speck of the lake."

"What lake?"

He chuckled. "*The* lake. Lake Michigan."

"Ah." She huddled into the big coat as cold wind slipped over her cheeks. He continued to guide them along the narrow through-way, and presently the channel widened, and George gasped as they suddenly found themselves on a huge body of open water. Moonlight sparkled on its surface.

Macon stopped rowing and they sat in silence for a while.

"Makes," George started hesitantly. She wasn't sure she wanted to know any more than she already did. She didn't even really know why she said his name, and her next words surprised her even as she said them. "I believe you." Some black growth inside her that remained bound up in darkness for all those years broke apart and dissolved.

Macon grunted quietly, then sniffed. "Thank you." He answered, his voice thick and gruff. "I appreciate you saying that."

They floated in silence for a long time, passing the thermos back and forth intermittently until the coffee was almost gone. Only the sound of the water lapping against the nearby shore and their vessel, the knock of the rope tapping against the side of the boat, and the cry of a single loon, somewhere in the distance, broke the deep silence of the night. George felt the tension drain from her body as she looked out over the dark water. Tattered clouds began to move across the face of the moon and Macon picked up the oar.

"Storm's comin'," he commented. He angled them back toward the shore and into the narrow channel.

The clouds had already blotted out the moon and all the stars by the time they got back to Macon's pond, and George shivered as the wind picked up.

"Two times you've been up and both times there's been hellacious weather. You're a storm-bringer, Peaches," Macon said as he rowed them back toward their starting point. "Didn't you have a song about that?" He looked up for a second, thinking, then his voice – the kind that gets right up under the skin – echoed across the clearing as he sang a line from one of her old songs. "I was born unto the storm…"

She joined him for the next lines with the harmony. They both stopped, stunned at the perfectly complementary way in which the quality of their voices wrapped together and floated into the night.

"I can't believe you remember that song," she muttered. "That was like, a million years ago. Or at least another lifetime." She looked away.

"Mel loved that album. She used to play it every Sunday morning." He smiled at the memory. "Like three times in a row. That's my favorite track. I don't know if I always loved it or if I just have Stockholm Syndrome." He winked as they landed on the shore, then hopped out.

George laughed. It felt nice to laugh, and bittersweet to share a good memory of Melly with Macon. "She was like that with music. We went on a road trip to see some dude she was into, and I swear, she made me listen to the same song the whole way. Four hours! We made a game out of finding every vocal harmony possible and swore we'd record it in eight-part *a capella* when we got back."

Macon pulled the boat onto the rocks and extended his hand to help her out. "Definitely sounds like a Mel thing." He clung to her fingers for an extra beat and gave them a little tug. She looked up at his concerned expression as he released her hand. "You okay, Peach?"

"Yeah, Makes." She sighed. "Thanks for that. I feel a lot calmer now. How long were we gone?"

He looked at his watch. "Two hours. Only a couple more to go. I'm sure we can find something else to keep us occupied until your beau wakes up." He shoved his hands into his pockets and started trudging toward the house. George caught up and walked next to him. "Or is he your husband?" He gave her a playful nudge with his elbow. "You have so many rings on your fingers, I wasn't sure if any of them were significant."

"Fiancé," she clarified. George lifted her hand, so her rings glinted in the low light, and grinned. "You know, that's kinda the point. I started wearing these when I was bartending. Now, just because I like them. They were meant to confuse the eye and make people think I was attached."

Macon chuckled beside her. "Did it work? Did you get hit on less?"

She snorted. "Fuck no. Men are animals."

He laughed softly and they continued in silence until they reached the cabin. "What do you want to do now? I can go to my room and leave you alone if you need some space."

She entered the cabin, warm with the coals of the fire and still smelling of dinner's spices just as the first raindrops began to fall outside. He hurried in after her.

"No, I think I'd rather not be alone right now." She hung her coat by the fireplace and rubbed her arms. "I mean, unless you need your own alone time, which I totally get," she added quickly. "You don't have to take care of me, but I wouldn't mind company, is what I mean."

He shrugged. "Nah, I'm enjoying the rarity of it, myself."

"Can I hear the album?"

He sighed. "I hoped you weren't gonna ask, but I can't put it off forever, right?"

"Right," she agreed decisively. "So, what's the deal? Why are you having such a hard time with it?"

"Eh," he muttered. "You'll see." He disappeared for a few minutes in the small recording room, and she heard the thump of cables being dropped to the floor. He emerged with his laptop and the cans and set up on the coffee table. He handed her the headphones and waited until they were settled over her ears. She looked up at him expectantly, and he touched the spacebar.

13

Lacrimaire

(n.) The quiet ache felt when listening to music that speaks to parts of you that can't put into words, as if it's unraveling a sadness even you didn't know.

She didn't say a word until the last note of the album faded. She slowly took the headphones off and placed them carefully on the table, then looked up at him. "Macon."

He shifted nervously. "Yeah? What do you think?"

"Fuck." She couldn't think of anything else to say.

"Was that a good fuck or a bad fuck?"

"I'll be real with you. There are some spots where I can hear some other instrumentals and vocal harmonies, but not much. It's…" She tried to put on her professional face. "It's full. The lyrics are… I'm sorry, Makes."

His face fell.

"It's a masterpiece." She gently closed the laptop and leaned back against the couch cushions.

"Jesus, I thought you hated it." He exhaled heavily. "Why did you apologize just now? What were you about to say?"

"I apologized because I've been struck inarticulate by this work. I just can't even wrap my head around how good this is."

He exhaled and put his face in his hands for a few seconds before he raked his fingers over his beard and fell back next to her. "I thought you hated it," he said again. "The way you broke my heart for just a minute there…"

"I don't understand why you've been holding on to this. How long have you been finished?"

"Well, I'm not, see. You said it yourself; there's still something missing."

"I mean…" she held her palms out. "I'd release this. I just think you can squeeze a little more out of it."

"Okay. What are you hearing?"

"Do you have a speaker we can play this on?"

"Errr… yeah, in the studio. It'll be crowded in there, though."

She pushed off the couch and stood. "That's fine, let's go."

She tapped the drum rhythm on the table next to the laptop. "I'd like to come in with that harmony vocal on the upbeat." She leaned in and added a new track titled "G scratch vox" then pulled the mic in close and recorded her idea for him to work from. "I like it when the vocal line extends over that section with the triplets. And then let's do a key change. Like…" she added another sample track and recorded her thought.

"Ah, yeah, I see what you mean. Shit. That's really beautiful."

"I don't know if I mentioned it, but I love the kick sounding like a heartbeat through the bridge."

He looked pleased. "I'm glad that comes through. And I think the piece we were looking for, could it be fiddle?"

"It would be really nice alongside the banjo. But do we have a cellist?"

"I know a really good one down in Detroit who's probably

home from tour by now. I can give her a call and get down there for a session if she's around."

"I don't think I can live without cello on this album, now that I'm thinking about it," George said.

"Kizi's a brilliant session player. She could probably get through five or six tracks in a day. You're right, I don't think I can live without it now, either." Macon's face broke into a wide smile. George found her heart doing a little flip as she noticed the way he transformed when he was talking about music. "Damn, it's so good to have someone to talk with about this. Even the band hasn't heard it yet."

"I appreciate you being open to working with me on this." She forcefully pushed the unexpected flash of feeling for him aside and chided herself internally.

"Peaches, you have a real talent for this." He gestured at the computer. "I knew I was onto something, but I could tell it wasn't finished." Relief flashed over his face. "I feel like I'll actually be able to get it in by the deadline now."

It was almost 3AM before they emerged from the small room, where they'd been cramped together in front of the laptop.

"So, after I go back to Indy, use the scratch vocals I just did for reference and give it your own flavor. Vocals, instrumentals, whatever. You think you can get that done? It'll probably be about a week before I can get back here."

"Yep, no problem." He rubbed his hand over the back of his neck. "Damn, Peach. I hate to see you on this side of the business."

"What do you mean?" George frowned, wondering how their last couple hours of work ended on that note. "You said you liked what we were working on!" she said indignantly.

"No, I just meant, you – working for the label. You should be performing."

"No way in hell." She shook her head adamantly. "No more stages for me. I hated being on display, hated the crowds." She looked up at him and made an apologetic face. "Not that I'm judging anyone who enjoys it. It just wasn't in me. I wanted to make music enough to do it, but… no. I hated touring so much. I know that's kind of your thing."

His eyebrows shot up in surprise. "It's just my job, really. I don't know what else I'd do. Although…" He stopped. "Never mind. Anyway, seems like it's late enough to call your fiancé now, yeah?"

She pulled her phone out of her pocket and hissed when she saw how late it was. "Oh my god!"

Macon retreated to his bedroom, and she crawled up into the loft to dial Kato. His face popped up on screen wearing a wide smile, which abruptly faded when he saw how exhausted she looked.

"Hey, babe," he said cautiously. "What's wrong?"

"Aunt Carla died."

"Shit." He exhaled in a rush. "I'm so sorry. I thought you had more time."

"Me too. It's okay. I'm going back tomorrow to finish the funeral arrangements. It'll be Saturday."

"You up at the cabin?"

"Yeah. Macon's album is really good. I think we're in the home stretch. What have you been doing?"

A gorgeous twink with a mermaid-dyed fauxhawk appeared in frame and caught Kato's earlobe with his teeth. He wiggled his eyebrows mischievously and looked at the camera before disappearing again.

Kato smirked. "That's luna. They're just doing that because they know it's you." He turned his face and called out, "Not a good time, luna. I'll meet you at the café." Something unintelligible on his end, then he turned back to the screen. "Sorry, we're heading out for brunch before we go to the site."

"That's awesome, K. I hope everything's going well. I don't wanna keep you. Go join your co-conspirators and make great art."

He smiled softly. "You sure? I can stay and talk if you need an ear."

"I'm ok. Talk later. Love you."

"Love you."

She ended the call and rolled over on her back in the bed. She almost decided to stay up but remembered she wasn't in her twenties anymore and had a five-hour drive ahead of her. She put her phone on the charger and closed her eyes. The tapping of the rain on the roof put her out almost immediately.

She woke to bright sunshine reflecting off the warm wood ceilings and walls. The smell of coffee, eggs, and bacon hung in the air, and George's stomach growled. She sat up quickly and grabbed her phone, then exhaled in relief when she saw it was still only 8:30AM.

Macon stood in the kitchen below wearing an apron, humming as he finished making breakfast. He looked up and cocked an eyebrow as she looked over the rail. "Come on, get some food in you before you make that drive. I made bacon and onion scramble and picked some wild blueberries."

"Wow." George searched for words to cover her surprise.

"I appreciate this, Macon. Seriously. I'm so grateful for the extra time you took with me last night. And for this. You really didn't have to."

He finished plating breakfast before untying his apron and settling his large frame into one of the chairs. George climbed down the ladder and sat across from him.

"You get a chance to talk to your man this morning?"

"Yeeeeah." She looked down at her food. "He was on his way out to brunch with one of the artists he's working with, so we talked for like, less than two minutes. It felt a little deflating after everything we did to kill time."

Macon grunted. "You tell him your aunt died?"

"Yeah, but it's ok. He's working. I can't expect his whole team to stop because of this. It's not his problem anyway."

Macon finished chewing and sat back. "He's your partner. It's his problem. Who's gonna be at the funeral for you?"

"All the kids will be there. Aunt Carla's coven." She smiled sadly. "I think a lot of people will be there. She gave a lot of her time to the Narcotics Anonymous community. I think a lot of people loved her." George stopped talking and swallowed hard a few times as an unexpected wave of emotion passed over her.

"I'm sorry you're going through this."

George took a deep breath and steadied herself. The pinpricks of an impending panic attack began at her chest.

Don't think about it.

"I've been through this shit fourteen times in the last three years. If there's anything I know how to handle, it's death," she answered flippantly. "It's kinda what I'm known for." She took a deep breath and rose from the table. "Anyway, I'll just clean up my dishes and be out of your hair."

He stood quickly. "Don't sweat it, just get on the road. I loaded all of your stuff earlier."

"Oh," she said, and found herself blushing for some reason. "Thanks."

He pulled her car key out of his back pocket and offered it to her. "I'll see you in a week."

She nodded and left wordlessly, only looking back when she opened the door, to find him meeting her eyes with an intensity that made her blush again before she quickly shut the door behind her and ran to her car.

Etterath

(n.) The feeling of emptiness after a long and arduous process is finally over, which leaves you relieved that it's over but missing the stress that organized your life into a mission.

George woke to the sound of rain, and for a moment she thought she was back in the cabin. She'd been back for a week, and it felt like a month. She opened her eyes and sighed in disappointment to find herself under the thin quilt covering Aunt Carla's bed. She collapsed there the night before after coming back from dinner with Barbara and the boys.

She groaned and rubbed her forehead as she remembered the hushed conversation she had in the parking lot with Barbara after Michael and Jack were belted into the car.

They stood near the restaurant, a little too close to the dumpster. Barbara took her elbow and led her directly behind the car, where the kids wouldn't be able to see them. George looked up at the vertically stacked signs by the road and her nose twitched as the light smell of trash washed over them on a breeze.

"Georgia, honey, we need to have a little talk," Barbara said in a low voice. George looked at Barbara's face, but the woman couldn't seem to meet her eyes. Something cold unfurled in George's belly.

"We have a lawyer, and we already had an appointment with the judge who's handling the case."

"Oh?" George remembered saying, in a voice that seemed too high and light for how hard her heart was beating.

"They want the boys staying in that house. We talked to Carla about it before she passed. We're taking over the lease."

What was this woman even saying? This woman, who was the daughter-in-law-of-the-third-wife-of-the-boys'-grandfather.

Like, what?

George wondered if that made her anything other than a familiar face to the boys. There certainly wasn't any blood relation.

How is this happening?

George wondered why her aunt hadn't told her. She thought about how they would push out all of Aunt Carla's good smells and fill it with their unfamiliar ones. She didn't have any words to give back to the conversation. It was hard to concentrate on anything other than those signs. *Cheddar's. Michaels. Home Goods. AMC Theaters. Home Depot. Golden Corral. What a time to be alive.*

"The judge wants them going to their same school. Same doctors, all of it. They want as much normalcy preserved as possible." She finally looked up to meet George's eyes.

"Oh, I see," said George lamely. "But… the documents."

"Honey." Barbara laid a soft hand on George's shoulder. "That's not really how these things work."

"I have a good job. They'd be well cared for." It was the only thing of value she could offer up in her favor.

"I've raised three boys, honey. Kent and I can give them

a good home. We're ready to take this on. We already have Jack in therapy twice a week, and Michael's in tutoring so we can get him back on track at school." Barbara was only four years older than George, but suddenly she felt like a child being chided by an adult. She was out of her depth and her heart knew it. She didn't even know the boys were in therapy already. She didn't really know anything about them at all. A feeling of futility swept over her as she realized how underprepared and outclassed she was in this conversation. She could see Jack's shock of pale hair through the back window. She knew when to die on a hill, and this wasn't it.

George blinked several times quickly, then reached out with numb fingers and clasped Barbara's hand. She remembered shaking it and saying something to the effect of, "Thanks for taking care of everything. I appreciate you. Let me know how I can support." She stood and watched, after that, until Barbara's car pulled onto the main road and disappeared into traffic.

Everyone involved knew George wasn't moving back to fucking Greenwood, Indiana. She'd felt a mixture of relief and guilt at the decision being made for her. She wasn't sure if that made her a bad person, but her capacity was limited. With Kato in Sweden, it would be a terrible time to add two children who needed extensive therapy and medical support to her already full plate.

It felt wildly anticlimactic to hear the family court's decision after so much workup to this point. After George had already spent many, many long hours dissecting what life would look like with a slam cut into having two kids. After she'd already had at least fifty panic attacks over the matter. But George called the lawyer who drew up the papers she signed as soon as she got home. He explained that, with a local father claiming parental rights, there was no way to take the boys out of state. Even if he *was* in jail. Ultimately, Hannah never had the right to sign over her children to someone else. It was all just meant to be a stopgap between loss of custody and the foster system. There was nothing she could do. Her sudden lack of purpose and the feeling she wasn't quite sure why she came in the first place haunted her. It was like watching a stick of dynamite simply sputter out just as the wick closed in on the explosive.

Regardless of the impassable legal limitations, she still couldn't help feeling like she failed Hannah. Failed Aunt Carla. Failed the boys. She was a stone sinking into the mattress, heavy against the sheets, yet somehow still insubstantial, a husk of who she'd been five weeks ago when she left. She realized she'd only been eating once a day since she got back from Michigan. It was always a struggle to eat when she felt this way. She just wanted to stay between the covers and listen to the rain in the stormy, autumnal darkness.

But the funeral was today, and she was the person who handled things. After a few more minutes of feeling sorry for herself, she rolled out of bed and moved across the cold floor. She pushed on her slippers and walked into the dark kitchen to make coffee as she powered up her phone.

A notification on the messaging app she was using to communicate with Kato while he was in Europe caught her attention. She opened the app and tapped her finger against the screen several times. Her hand froze in midair just before the handle of the kitchen cabinet she was reaching for. The color drained from her face and her eyes went wide. Her phone dropped from boneless fingers onto the table, and she fell to her knees on the cold linoleum. She sat there for a few minutes. Then she leaned forward and pressed her forehead against the floor.

After shaking without sound or tears for several minutes, George leaned back on her heels and wiped her hands over her cheeks. No sense in getting all puffy and out of sorts ahead of the funeral. She sniffed and blew her nose then took a deep breath and stood. She made coffee, then grabbed a baggie and stuffed it with ice to take down the puffiness in her face.

Her heart felt like it was melting into her ribcage.

Everything will be fine, she told herself. This is fine.

Amentalio

(n.) The sadness of realizing that you're already forgetting
sense memories of the departed—already struggling to
hear their voice, picture the exact shade of their eyes, or
call to mind the quirky little gestures you once knew by
heart.

Though it didn't seem possible, Aunt Carla's funeral was
even more of a blur for George than Hannah's. She
knew she was handling things capably as she got everything
set up, but she watched herself do it all in third person.

*Go ahead and put the lemon squares in the kitchen, it's that way. Ask
Tanya when you get there. She's the pretty lady with gold glasses and
curly brown hair. Oh, thank you. Welcome. I've set the guest book up
near the entrance. Why don't you go add your name? I think everyone's
congregating in the room where the service will be held. The flowers need
to go into that room over there. Donations? No, but I have some sugges-
tions we can talk about later if you want` to leave me your email. Yes,
I still live in California. Yes, the boys are fine. They're with Barbara,
they've already arrived. Thank you for your condolences. Thank you
for your kind words. Thank you. Thank you. Thank you. Thank you.
Thank you. Thank you for coming. I'm sorry for your loss, too.*

She moved toward the front row and turned to settle into

her chair, which was flanked by the boys and Carla's coven. Just as she was turning to sit, a movement caught her eye, and she turned to see a beautiful, broad-chested man with a sharply trimmed, short beard, wearing an expensive, tailored suit, sit down in the back row. She did a double-take and her eyes shot up to meet his piercing blue ones for a brief moment before she sat.

How? She thought. *How is he here?*

By the time she finished talking to the boys and Little Helen after the service, Macon was nowhere to be seen. George wondered if she'd dreamed the whole thing.

She went through the gauntlet of condolences in a trance and finally escaped to the same planter in the back of the mortuary where she found solitude at Hannah's funeral. Her grandparents' services were held here, too, and her dad's before that. And Henry's before that. And… so many others that the staff at the mortuary knew her by sight and name.

Too many funerals.

She held no real hope of finding anything, but she checked the spot where she last found the cigarettes just in case. "No fucking way," she muttered as her fingers found a pack. She withdrew it and was relieved to see it was new. She took a cigarette and the lighter within and lit it gratefully before leaning back against the cold brick wall. She closed her eyes and exhaled.

"Smoking? With a killer voice like that? *Tsk.*"

George's eyes flew open and she nearly vaulted herself into outer space as Macon's voice intruded on her moment. She hadn't even heard him approach.

"Shit, you scared the crap out of me, Macon." Her body

was still reacting to being startled, but she immediately felt glad for his presence. Confused, but grateful, nonetheless.

"Gimme a drag," he said with a small smile.

She huffed a little laugh and passed it to him. "What on earth are you doing here, Macon? How'd you find me?"

"I just called the label and told them I wanted to send flowers for the funeral." He put the cigarette to his lips, then passed it back to her.

"You sent flowers?" She looked up at him as she pinched it between her fingers and took another drag.

"Fuck no. Dealing with all those shitty, white funeral flowers was the bane of my goddamn existence when Mel died. I never want to smell another fucking lily for the rest of my life."

"Yeah, I know what you mean." George's face lifted for a moment with a smile. She was silent for a second. "But why did you come?"

"You can't let people go through something like this without support."

"It's a five-hour drive!"

"Yeah. But it's the least I could do. You're really going through it, Peaches. You've landed square in the shit."

She sighed and closed her eyes again as she leaned against the wall. "You have no fucking idea, Macon. My whole life is falling apart right now." She put her hands over her face as an unexpected sob broke free. "I'm sorry." She dabbed the corner of her eye with a tissue from her pocket.

"Jesus, Georgia. Why are you apologizing?" He ran a hand over the back of his neck. "This is the second funeral you're attending in less than a month. This whole situation is pretty fucked."

"It's not just this," she said quietly. "I don't even know how to talk about what's going on."

"Then sit with me. Talk to me. That's why I came." He moved toward the door and motioned her over. "When I was looking for you, I found a couple empty rooms with couches. We can go grab some waters and find a little quiet space."

"I really should get back to everyone." She sighed heavily.

"Hey, Georgia? In case no one reminded you, you're allowed to grieve, too. It's okay. Everyone in there can take care of themselves for little while."

"Why are you so good at this?" George frowned as she gave in and moved toward the door.

He shrugged as he opened it for her. "Working the steps. Being a sponsor. Growing the fuck up, finally."

They sat on a yellow couch in a room with unnervingly large, mustard-colored flowers on the wallpaper. A few wingback chairs sat around a small coffee table. The lights were low and indoor plants softened the space.

"Okay, so if it's not this…" Macon gestured at their setting. "What is it?"

She told him about the boys, the legal situation, then paused. "That's part of it, and this is the other." She sighed and pulled her phone from the pocket of her black dress. She brought up the message she received from the unknown number, the one that sent her to her knees. She held it up for him to see and pressed play on the video. Macon's eyebrows shot up as noises of carnal pleasure emanated softly from the phone.

"So, that…" She pointed to the face in the forefront of the

video. "That's my fiancé, Kato," she said conversationally. "And the beautiful twink with their cock in his ass is luna, an artist he's working with."

"Shiiiiit," he breathed. "I'm so sorry." Macon covered his mouth with his hand.

"Funny thing is, Makes…" She stared into a spot on the wall and paused. "I was hurt for, like, five minutes. And I mean that literally. Then I just went numb. And there's something in the back of my mind that feels like relief."

"Yeah, some of that is probably trauma, George. You're in shock."

Mmm, she hummed.

She leaned back against the cushion and moved closer to him, enjoying the heat pulsing off his body. He leaned back too, and they sat in comfortable silence for almost half an hour, broken only by Macon periodically passing George a bottle of water to sip. George finally sat up and took a deep breath.

"This quiet way you have about you is very healing, Macon. Thank you. Again. I feel way more grounded now. But I really should be getting back to everyone." She gave him a regretful look. "Though honestly, I'd prefer to sit in here with you in silence until everyone is gone."

"Are you coming home – to my home, I mean…" He shook his head and started over. "Will you be back at the cabin Monday, or do you still have a lot to do here?"

"No, I'll be back Monday afternoon. There's not much left for me here. You want a place to stay tonight so you don't have to drive back in the dark? Aunt Carla's place has an extra bedroom."

He thought for a few seconds and heaved a sigh before

answering. "Nah, I'll head back tonight." He took her hand and gave it a soft squeeze before standing and helping her up. "Come here." He opened his arms and George fell into them. He wrapped her up and gave her a hard squeeze before releasing her and taking her hand. "Go deal with your people. I'll see you in a couple days."

She let her hand trail out of his as he turned and walked away. He gave her a backward glance and a small smile that did something strange to her stomach as he disappeared through the door. As she exited and headed back toward the communal room, Tanya fell into stride next to her and bumped her arm.

"Who was *that*?" she asked in a conspiratorial tone.

Georgia grinned. "Business acquaintance. He's the musician I told y'all about that I'm up here working with."

"Mm hmm," Tanya said. "I can tell by the way you're blushing he's a business acquaintance."

George burst out laughing, and she felt a bloom of warmth wash over her cold body. She hardly knew this woman, but she felt like long-lost family, and the feeling was very welcome at the moment. The whole coven, but especially Tanya, had taken good care of her in the week leading up to this shit-tastic day. "He used to date my best friend," she explained. "I feel like that'd be weird. Even, you know, if I was interested. Which I'm not."

"How long ago?" Tanya asked. George answered that it was fifteen years in the past and Tanya scoffed at her. "Girl," she said. "Everyone's a different person by now. That's not weird at all." She smacked George's arm lightly. "He's freakin' gorgeous. Jeez Louise."

Mmm, George hummed. "I guess he does clean up alright.

Last time I saw him, his beard was down to his chest, and he's usually in flannel with, like, an axe in his hand. Very lumberjack-y vibes. I almost didn't recognize him when he showed up today."

"God, that's hot," Tanya commented. "He looks like a model, but I'd probably like the mountain man version of him even more. Also, he's like eight-feet tall, what's up with that? Men who look like that only exist in smutty books." She fanned her face melodramatically and George giggled.

She'd avoided dwelling too much about his looks since he reentered her life. But once Tanya said it, it was all she could think about.

16

Drisson

(n.) An unexpected twinge of attraction for a friend; a
flutter of desire you don't necessarily want to feel.

Macon stretched his arms over his head and groaned as
he unfolded himself from the hunched position he'd
taken in front of the laptop.

"Let's get out of here for a few minutes and take a walk. I
need to stretch my legs and get some sunshine while there's
still some to be had. You brought another storm on your tail,
Peach. We might get snow tonight."

"Damn, really? Will I be able to drive out on Wednesday?
I have to go sign some papers for the estate attorney in Indy.
I was planning on leaving Wednesday morning, hanging out
with the boys on Thursday, and heading back up here at the
end of the week to wrap up."

"I don't think it'll stick. Ground's still too warm. You'll be
okay. But I still need some air right now."

"Okay, I could use a break, too."

They bundled up and made their way past the pond before
heading into the thick woods at the far side of the fairy ring.

George picked her way past a large fern and ducked
under a branch. "So, I never really asked – this is a vacation
rental, but you live here. What's the deal?" She pulled out
her phone and snapped several pictures of an interesting,

moss-covered branch.

Macon easily stepped over a fallen log with his long legs. "It's my land, my house. My granddad left it to me when he died. It was a vacation rental before I decided to live here full time, and I still rent it out sometimes when I go on tour."

"Alright," George panted as she clambered awkwardly over the log. "I won't tell." She went down on one knee to take a picture of a good mushroom sprouting from the pine litter.

Macon laughed. "I don't care if you tell the label. I licensed a couple of my songs a while back. I'm not fuck-off rich, but I'm far from hurting. The royalties will take care of me indefinitely."

"I was watching TV one night and lost my damn mind when I heard one of your songs. That was before I worked for the label."

"Yeah, I had a couple placements in series, and another one was licensed for a car commercial. Just a couple of those earned more than all my album sales combined. Point is, I don't need the money the label is paying me to stay in my own house. The point was kinda more 'stickin' it to the man,' you know?"

She laughed. "Well, like I said, I won't tell."

"You still have a little rebel in there somewhere. I see her, Peach," he teased. "What do I have to do to set her free?"

"Sorry to disappoint, but I threw away the key to her cage a long time ago." George took several steps backward to photograph a picturesque clump of berries and let out a squeal as she fell into a fern. She settled face first into the soggy plant with one leg over her head, still stuck on the branch. "Ouch," she said in a muffled voice.

Macon stifled a laugh and doubled back to hoist her back

to her feet.

"Rude!" George scowled. "I hurt my knee."

"How did this even happen?" He sighed as he pulled a fern frond from her hair.

"I got distracted," she admitted with a defeated gesture.

"With your phone," he said with a smirk, and her scowl deepened. "Let's see." He helped her in a sitting position on a log and probed the joint through her jeans. He followed her hisses and ouches with his fingers. "Yeah, it's swollen. There's already a little fluid behind it. Let's get you back."

He supported her as she hobbled back in the direction of the cabin. After a few minutes of painfully slow progress, he huffed an impatient sigh. "Georgia, it's gonna be a lot faster if I carry you."

She noticed he always called her by her given name when he was about to start ordering her around.

"What if we make a crutch out of wood? Like out of some sticks?" she suggested.

His mouth quirked in amusement, and he gestured widely at the trees around them. "Go ahead."

"Well, *I* don't know how."

"Just let me carry you, Georgia."

"I'm too heavy!"

He made a skeptical face. "I've carried armloads of firewood heavier than you."

"You can't!"

"I damn well can," he said, and he swept her up into his arms before she could argue anymore. George clapped her mouth shut and turned bright red as he turned and began to stalk back to the cabin. She looked straight ahead, silently, and tried not to notice his breath on her cheek.

George was sleeping soundly when a cacophony startled her awake in the deep black of night. The wind howled above her, and it took several long seconds to realize the stovepipe had fallen in, and a gout of smoke was pouring from the opening atop the wood burning stove below. Another look upward, and she realized the roof was open to the sky, and the edges were softly glowing with fire. She squealed in alarm.

"Macon!" she yelled as she tried to scramble off the couch. She hissed as an electric bolt of pain shot up from her knee. Rain and snow blew in through the hole above.

Macon burst from his room, his hair and eyes wild, in his thermals, and surveyed the damage briefly before springing into action. He covered the smoking hole on the stove with an iron skillet, then shoved on his boots, grabbed his coat, and disappeared out the door. The wind howled and Georgia heard thumping on the roof. Something dark covered the hole and the snow and rain stopped blowing into the cabin.

Macon finally blew back in on a frigid gust; frozen water still caught in his beard and eyebrows. His thermals were soaked and he was shivering uncontrollably. He stood near the stove, which was still generating some heat from the coals, and stripped down to his tight white underwear. George realized she was gaping and shut her mouth quickly.

"Fuck," he muttered. He disappeared into his room and returned a few seconds later wearing a thick robe and perched on the edge of the couch to pull off his sodden socks. He finished hanging out his coat and clothes, and he perched his boots near the stove to dry. He finally stopped and plopped down on the couch.

He leaned back against the cushions wearily. "What time is it?"

"2AM," answered George. "Are you okay?"

He grunted. "Yeah, I'm fine. I managed to get a tarp stapled in place for tonight, but I'll have to fix it tomorrow morning when there's some light. I almost slid off twice." He glanced at the stove. "It's gonna be a cold night." He looked over at her and searched her face. "If you get too cold, come sleep with me."

She blushed and looked away, then felt his hand on her arm.

"I mean it, Georgia. It's already like fifty-five degrees in here and we lost all the heat up in the rafters when that hole opened up. We obviously can't get the fire going again until the chimney's reattached. If you get too cold, come share body heat with me. That's all."

"Alright," she murmured.

"I'm going back to bed," he said wearily. "I'll see you in the morning."

George was shivering when she woke up. It was still more dark than light, and she looked at her phone. 5:05AM. The wind still howled outside. Her teeth chattered, and in the low light, thick clouds puffed out from her lips. Macon wasn't kidding when he said it would be cold. She wondered how the mild, late autumn weather they'd enjoyed just the day before had shifted to this so quickly.

Her breath whistled as her lungs tightened in the cold air. She snuggled as deeply as she could into the comforter, but she could hardly feel her feet, and her ass was a block of ice.

After ten minutes of trying to get comfortable, she finally

had enough. She rose from the couch on the cold pillars of her legs and held onto its frame as she hobbled toward Macon's room.

This is a stupendously terrible idea, she thought as she turned the knob and pushed the door open. But she was cold enough that she didn't care. Now that she was in his room, however, with the faint shape of his huge form covered with a pile of blankets and breathing evenly before her, she was at a loss. It seemed rude to wake him. But maybe even more rude just to crawl into his bed without permission? This was such a gray area. She shifted from foot to foot and the wood plank flooring beneath her groaned softly. Macon's breath hitched and he rolled over.

"You okay, Peach?" came his voice softly from the darkness.

"Yeah," she said. She was relieved he wasn't freaked out to find her watching him while he slept, and even more relieved she didn't have to prod him awake to ask if she could come to bed with him. "I'm just really cold."

"Come on." He lifted the edge of the comforter, and she needed no extra encouragement to climb in quickly. She tried to stay a polite distance from him once she was settled, but he pulled her in against his chest. "Once you're good, you can sleep wherever you want, but warm up for a few minutes. You're freezing."

She didn't argue and snuggled gratefully back into the soft terrycloth of his robe. She let out her breath in relief as the tremoring in her muscles finally ceased. Soon, he was breathing evenly again, but his arm remained around her. She wiggled a little closer to him, enveloped in his masculine scent, and thought fretfully that she probably wouldn't be able to get back to sleep under these conditions.

George woke to the sound of hammering above and decided to stay in bed. It would never cease to amaze her, how easily she was able to sleep in this place. She hadn't slept this much, or this deeply, in over twenty years. Her knee still throbbed when she flexed her leg, and she suspected that even to ask if she could offer help would be an unneeded distraction. She propped her pillow up and looked out the small window in Macon's bedroom. Outside was still gray and howling, but significantly brighter. Luminous, white snow covered everything she could see, and the trees beyond the clearing whipped their bare branches with every gust, stripped of their autumn leaves in the night by the storm.

She was dozing with her phone in her hand when Macon finished and came back inside. She heard the stomp of his boots as he knocked the snow off, then he appeared in the doorway in his sock feet, looking red and windswept.

"Call the lawyers and tell them you need to reschedule. You're not getting out of here tomorrow. A new storm system blew in and we're about to get dumped on."

"Fuck me, are you serious? I thought you said it would be melted!" George groaned.

He shrugged. "I don't make the weather."

"Sorry. I'm just... this is a shit time to be stuck. My signal's almost non-existent with this storm. Or maybe it's just this room. I wasn't expecting to get trapped here. I'm not sure if I can get any messages out."

He held out his hand for the phone, and she gave it to him with a questioning look. He disappeared for a few seconds, then returned. "You can still get enough signal to get your texts out from the loft. You compose. I send."

She laughed. "Are you serious?"

"Do you have a better idea?" He eyed her knee, then met her eyes again. "I suppose you could wrap your legs around my head and sit on my shoulders," he suggested with a straight face.

George blushed. "First way is fine," she said quickly, to his clear amusement. She tapped out a message and handed him the phone.

He disappeared and returned a few seconds later. "Next."

She giggled. "Alright." She tapped out another message, and within a few minutes of back-and-forth, contacted everyone she needed to. He handed her phone back and she shook her head. "I don't know why you're being so nice to me."

"Would you do the same for me?"

"Of course."

"Why don't you think you deserve the same?"

"God, Macon. Do you moonlight as a therapist, or something? Because you sound exactly like mine." She laughed lightly.

He continued to look at her with a serious, questioning gaze. "I actually mean it. This isn't hypothetical. I'm asking you why you don't believe you're worthy of the same treatment you'd give to others."

"I just don't want to be a burden. I think help should be saved for people who really need it. And I don't."

He cocked an eyebrow and smirked. "Keep telling yourself that, Peaches."

"Unghhhh," she groaned. She changed the subject. "What are we supposed to do all day?"

"We could work on the album?"

"Right, of course," she answered. "Lemme hear what you did while I was gone."

"Stay here," he ordered, and left the room to get his laptop.

They spent the rest of the day listening to the new additions to the tracks, and George didn't even stop to think about how inappropriate it was for her to be in his bed, with him propped up on the headboard next to her, as they worked. Connecting with Macon felt like the rekindling of a decades-old friendship, even though that relationship never existed. But there was something deeply familiar and comforting about him that had her abandoning all sense of propriety.

17

Rasque

(n.) A moment you instantly wish you could take back,
feeling a pulse of dread right after crossing the point
of no return. Wanting to take just one step backward
in time, reverting to the way things used to be, in the
halcyon days of just a minute ago.

Water dripped from the roofline of the cabin, and somewhere the crash of snow as it spilled from a branch into a wet drift reached George's ears as she sat in the driver's seat of the car. Macon was leaning down, talking to her through the open window.

"I'll be back in two days." She looked up at him and felt something sad twinge in her chest. "And then we'll be wrapped, and I'll be out of your hair for good. Back to LA with your opus."

He pursed his lips. "I wish you didn't have to go. We hit a really good flow with the music."

She blushed. "Well, I'm sure you'll be glad to have your solitude back. And have all my drama out of your life," she chuckled self-consciously. "I know I would."

"I don't mind," he said with a slight shrug. "But I know you need to get back. I can't keep you out here in the woods in this broke-down, fuckin' cabin just because you're my favorite producer."

She laughed lightly and the corners of his mouth turned

up.

He straightened and smacked the roof of the car. "Go on now, git." He grinned as she rolled up the window. "Drive safe."

She caught sight of him as she was about to turn out of view, standing in the drive with his hand lifted in a farewell wave. There was a moment back there in which the urge to kiss him goodbye almost overtook her, and she was glad she hadn't broken that barrier between them. For one, she was leaving. Two, she was clearly broken as fuck. Three, it would be entirely unacceptable to throw herself at the talent. It was probably a fire-able offense, even for her. And fourth, but certainly not the least of her reasons: she wasn't sure if she could stop once she crossed that line.

The next two days passed uneventfully. She met with the estate lawyers, took the boys to lunch, and went with them to visit the tree they planted for Hannah. She met with Tanya for coffee and finished boxing up the rest of Aunt Carla's house. As she signed the legal papers, she thought of Macon's music. When she picked at her sandwich, she thought of him cooking down below as she waited in the warm loft bed. Mid-conversation she drifted off, thinking of all the ways his face had of turning into a smile when he was talking about music.

In between the busy moments, she put all her focus into getting through the crates and crates of physical photos Carla left behind. It was a special hell for her, flipping through each photo, knowing she was the sole bearer of the memories for all of them now.

She sat at Aunt Carla's kitchen table. She ran her fingers

over the surface of it, probably, she thought, for the last time. This table, like her grandparents, her dad, all her cousins, and now her aunt, had been a part of her life as far back as she could remember. Like them, it would soon be just one more memory.

She couldn't wait to get the fuck out of Indiana. She wasn't sure she'd ever come back after this. Nothing good came from this place. It seemed all this land could offer was wave upon wave of sorrow.

She pulled out her phone and tapped out a message.

I guess we should talk, she wrote, as she forwarded the video to Kato. *At this point, it's not super urgent. Take your time to process, as I have. Let me know when. I'll be back in LA by Saturday, so after that? Anyway, hope you're well, and that the install is going smoothly.*

Even with the cold, hard evidence of his infidelity staring her in the face, she wanted to make sure he was still okay. She shook her head in disgust.

What the hell is wrong with me?

But she already knew. She thought back to Macon's words about Mel — *worst thing I did to her was that I stayed.* She thought maybe that was true of her relationship with Kato. They'd been cooling off since the early days, even though their friendship deepened. They'd been engaged for six of the ten years they'd been together. If she wanted to get married, she probably would have tried to get a wedding together some-where during that stretch of time. But other things were prioritized, and that alone should have told her something important. Things like co-ownership of the condo made the logistics of a breakup feel impossible with her busy schedule.

She felt the familiar, tingling weight in her chest and strug-gled to catch her breath. She thought of Macon putting her in the boat, and she went outside. *Touch grass,* she thought, and she kicked off her shoes. She wandered through the cold, dead grass of the backyard, examining all the little trinkets and sculptures Aunt Carla had tucked away between the brown foliage. She pulled an iron windchime shaped like an owl from a hook near the door and went inside to get ready to leave this house for the last time. For the last trip up to Michigan. The last time she'd see Macon. Maybe she'd kiss him goodbye this time, when there was nothing left at stake.

She was four hours into the drive when Lucia's number came up on her dash.

"Hey, babe!" Lucia greeted her cheerfully. "First of all, can I just say: you are a goddamned genius and I love you. Thank you for getting this done, despite everything you're dealing with."

"Okay… what are we talking about?"

"I just listened to the tracks!"

George was silent, her brows drawn together. "What tracks?"

"George, where's your head? Ben Macon's tracks. He sent the links this morning."

"O-Oh!" George stuttered as she tried to think of something intelligent to say. "I'm sorry, I didn't know he was sending those. I'm actually headed back up there now, and I thought we still had some stuff to finish up. I'm just really surprised."

"Ah, well. He told me you said the label was getting nervous and wanted proof of life." George could hear the grin in Lucia's voice. "So, he sent us three tracks."

George relaxed. "That's great. It's also exciting that I can talk to you about it because… hello. It's eleven songs that all have single potential, Lucia. It's the best album I've heard in a decade. You're gonna shit when you hear the rest. Which ones did he send?"

"Lemme pull up the songs, hold on. Okay, he sent *Went to Pieces*. Gorgeous, just gorgeous. Hashtag sad-girl-summer. May release."

"I was legit thinking the same thing," George agreed enthusiastically. "Okay, what next?"

"*Together*."

"Oh, I love that one. I feel like that could be next year's big wedding song if we release the single at the right time. Valentine's Day or before?"

"I hear it too, George. Definite 'first dance' material. Maybe January, give it some time to percolate."

"Take that, Alex Warren," George muttered smugly, and Lucia chuckled.

"The last one he sent will be this season's breakup song. We can release it ahead of the full album. Always popular, especially in the winter. Annnd…" Lucia paused to look at her notes. "That one is… *You, the Storm*."

"*You, the Storm*?" George muttered. "Which one is that?"

"That's the one with the line 'you live for the tempest, and I live alone,'" Lucia sang. "Umm… she's basically a hot mess but he wants to be with her, she leaves him, he falls apart." She snorted on the other end of the call. "You know – the typical, romantic, sad shit people love. It's really good, though. Bitches gonna be crying to this all season. I'm almost wondering if we should make this our first drop or save it for next year. We'll definitely want the full album to drop after the new year."

"That's so weird," George murmured. "I literally have no idea which song you're talking about. I'll ask Macon about it when I get back up there."

"I am so pleased, George. If the rest of it is as good as you say, this is going to be something we're all really proud of. He's giving you co-producer credit beside his name, did you know that?"

"No," George faltered. "He didn't tell me."

"Well, he just loves working with you. He communicated nothing but glowing praise for your efforts. Oh, and by the way, I wanna know who the absolute smoke show is on backup."

"Macon did all his own backing tracks."

"Are we listening to the same album?" Lucia laughed incredulously. "I'm talking about the female harmony on Together and Went to Pieces. I don't know who she is, but you can tell she's hot. I want all the details."

"Right, right," she murmured. Heat rose in George's cheeks. "Hey listen, Lucia. I'm about to hit a stretch of the road where I won't have any signal. I'll get back to you as soon as I'm done with Macon."

"No problem, babe. Again, congratulations."

"Thanks, boss." Georgia was almost hyperventilating by the time she was able to end the call. She pulled onto the shoulder and closed her eyes until her breath steadied. She had been so careful not to let her past life seep into her current one. She couldn't believe Macon gave them the files with her vocals.

She finally pulled back onto the highway, her teeth ground together, and her knuckles white on the steering wheel.

She boiled out of the car and slammed the door. She'd had the last hour to get herself good and worked up, and by the time she turned onto the long drive off the highway, she was on fire.

Macon stepped out of the cabin and began to walk toward her as she stalked in his direction.

"What the actual fuck, Macon?" she yelled as soon as she was near. Macon swept past her and continued walking toward the pond. He reached the edge and shoved his hands into his coat pockets. She turned and stomped after him. He turned to face her when she reached the edge of the water, and his face was icy. "I can't believe you gave Lucia the tracks with my vocals, Macon. You crossed a line."

His lips pressed tightly together. "Did you know the label was planning on dropping me before they heard the new tracks, Georgia?"

Uh oh. She froze, suddenly understanding why his face looked like it did. "No," she began, then she paused as she remembered Lucia saying it would be his last album. She looked up sheepishly. "Maybe they said something about that before I left."

"You're so caught up, you didn't even stop to think how that would feel for me. To find out from someone else."

"First of all, Macon – it wasn't my news to give."

"Fuck that, Georgia. I'm not just another artist. Don't you dare pretend we're not more than that to each other."

Her phone buzzed in her hand, and she glanced down at it.

He made an impatient, irritated noise. "You, in the context of this job, are a fucking nightmare. Constantly looking at your phone. Always checking social media, your email.

You're in a near constant state of dissociation."

She recoiled in anger. "Dissociation? Rich, coming from you."

"The fuck does that mean?"

"Not all of us managed to make enough money to leave the world behind, Macon. You, up here existing outside of reality, not letting anyone contact you… Then you look me in the face and tell me I spend too much time working. The privilege of it makes me sick. I have to fight for my place every day."

"I've worked hard for what I have, too, George." His neck muscles flexed as he clenched his jaw.

"Sure, but you're in a different place now, and you don't seem to realize it."

"I can't believe you're mad at me because I'm in a place where I can finally take care of myself." He shot her a look of incredulous anger.

"I mean, of course you're calm. Of course you're fine. You don't have to participate in life with the rest of us anymore."

He shook his head angrily. "Go home, Georgia. Go get your reward for handling me. I'll send the files back to the real world as soon as I can. Enjoy LA."

"I'm not going anywhere until you acknowledge that what you did was messed up. You don't even know what you've done!" She stomped her foot. Her phone buzzed and she glanced at it quickly before she shoved it back in her pocket. "You had no right to do it without my consent."

"You can't even have a fight without looking at that fucking thing," he said with a smirk.

"What? *This thing?*" She yanked the phone from her pocket and held it up. "My *phone?* *Fuck* this phone." She used all her strength to hurl it into the pond, where it disappeared with a pronounced, wet *plop* into the water. Macon drew his breath in sharply and his eyebrows shot up. She stood, stunned, as the water rippled outward. She couldn't believe she'd just done it, but she couldn't take it back now. "You want me to go home? Fine."

She turned on her heel and stomped back to the car. Wind whipped her hair as she got behind the wheel. Another storm was coming.

She was five minutes down the road from Macon's when she finally broke down. The indie music channel she was listening to on satellite radio played the opening notes of the exact song she wanted, and she was ugly crying by the time she cranked up the music and howled along to the chorus.

"Michigan's in the rear-view nowwwww, put your hands where I can see-ummm… You took the words right out of my mouuuuuuth, when you knew that I would need-um-mmmm…" Her voice broke as tears ran down her face.

She sped down the highway, singing along with every sad song she could catch. She was a mere fifteen minutes down the road when a tremor started that she could feel under the gas pedal and, within minutes, the whole car was shuddering ominously.

"Oh my god," she muttered with a sniffle. "How are you breaking down? You're only like a year old, you piece of absolute shit." The rental sputtered to a stop on the shoulder, and she took a moment to breathe. *What a stupid time to throw my phone in a lake.* She looked around the dash. Didn't all these new cars have roadside assistance? She scrolled through the choices on the dash display until she found OnStar, only to discover the account wasn't set up or connected.

She laughed hysterically as she sat behind the wheel. She hadn't seen another car the whole time she'd been on the road. She had to be at least ten or twelve miles from Macon's property, but the closest town, she knew, was another twenty miles past that. She laughed until her abs were cramping. She wanted to cry. She had to go back to his house. She dug around in her suitcase until she found her trainers and slipped them on, then pulled on her coat.

Gonna be a long walk, she thought. *A long, long walk of shame.*

Macon stood by the pond staring unseeingly at the woods beyond. He didn't really know why he was so mad at her. And he didn't quite understand why she was so mad at him. All he knew was that he'd spent the entire week, since Sunday, with a pain in his stomach. And the closer it got to today, the worse he felt. He could only think that this was the last two days he'd probably ever spend with her. He couldn't see any scenario in which they would work, and he wasn't sure why he felt so broken up about it.

He chewed his lip as he looked at the intermittent raindrops that were beginning to ripple the surface of the pond. He almost toppled over from shock when she threw her phone in the water. He couldn't help but grin at it now that he'd been standing in the cold, cooling off for a good, long while. He remembered the moment of shock and regret on her face. The sound of it hitting the water. He bit his lip now, to keep from laughing.

What a ridiculous fucking mess of a woman, a piece of him said. The other half flared at the insult. *She feels like home,* it replied. He grunted and started back toward the cabin.

His brow creased. He hoped she got far enough south to avoid the storm before it hit. The weather report predicted flurries, but the glowering clouds rolling in said otherwise. He looked up at the sky as the rain turned to ice.

George's voice was hoarse from yelling. She'd been trudging along the edge of the highway, very vocally letting out her frustrations to the impassive forest. And now it had begun to snow in earnest, and she was sure she was still at least six miles from Macon's driveway, itself nearly a mile from the road to the house. She'd finally burned out her anger and moved on to the self-reflection phase of her meltdown about half a mile back. Her lungs constricted painfully as a blast of arctic air cut straight down the roadway and blasted her in the face. She stopped to pull her scarf over her mouth and bumped up her pace to a jog. She thought she might have enough juice in her to run all the way there. She dropped into the fastest pace she thought she could maintain and began to run.

Macon sat on the couch in the warm glow of the fire and the many candles he'd tucked around the main room. He usually saved them in case the electricity went out, but tonight he needed some primal comfort. Being surrounded by all the tiny points of flame soothed his anger and cooled the throbbing bruise of his heartache. He held a book loosely in his hands as he stared out the window at the blue dusk. The snow blew sideways.

"Macon!" George screamed, but the wind tore away her voice and sent it scattering into the trees. She was close to his cabin, she knew. She could smell the smoke from his fire intermittently, when the wind blew right. But she couldn't see much, and it would be completely dark soon. She called his name again, best she could with stinging vocal chords and ever-tightening lungs.

Macon threw on his coat and boots and stood near the door, listening. He could have sworn he heard someone calling for help between the howling of the wind. Again, a small, unintelligible voice came to him on a gust. He opened the door and stepped into the storm.

George stumbled over something unseen, hidden beneath the thick blanket of snow that already accumulated in the three hours since she left her car. The rubber bottoms of her running shoes slipped, and she went careening into a wet drift. She gasped as snow breached the front of her coat and a chunk went sliding down her chest, leaving a trail of ice water in its wake. She pushed herself out of the drift and beat the packed ice from her jeans and coat. She was soaking wet. A deep, convulsive shiver hit her. *Maybe I should sit down. No, no, that's the wrong answer. That's how I almost died before.*

She slipped again and sat down heavily in the snow. She buried her face in her scarf and shut her eyes against the stinging gusts of ice. Suddenly she found herself being heaved up as big hands gripped under her armpits. They yanked her off her feet, cradled her against a hard chest, and carried her directly into the screaming wind.

Mamihlapinatapai

(n.) A look shared between two people, each wishing that the other would initiate something they both desire but which neither wants to begin.

George's lips were blue and her whole body was stiff as a board, locked in one, prolonged muscle contraction, by the time Macon got her back to the cabin. He kicked the door shut behind him and carried her to the wood stove. He stopped close enough to feel the heat radiating off in waves and held her until her rigid muscles eased and she was merely wracked with deep shivers.

He looked down into her face, his mouth inches from hers. "We have to stop meeting like this," he murmured.

Her eyes fell to his mouth, and he cleared his throat before setting her on her feet. He peeled off his coat and tossed it on the couch, then turned to George, who stood shivering and miserable, her teeth chattering and her hair plastered against her head.

"Take off your clothes, Georgia. Stand as close to the stove as you can. I'm gonna go start a bath so we can get your body temperature up."

She nodded and slowly began removing her clothing, but she was sopping wet and her limbs weren't working as they should. She heard the tap turn on and a few seconds later,

Macon emerged from his room with a thick towel. He went to one knee to help her undress. He was businesslike and quick about it, and when she was down to her underwear, he wrapped the towel around her and helped her as she walked haltingly to the tub.

She dropped the towel and gripped the edge of the porcelain.

"Georgia," Macon said softly. "This is gonna hurt. You need to stay in." He lifted her off her feet and slowly lowered her into the water. She cried out as the heat made fiery pin-pricks all over her body, none worse than in her hands and feet. She was admirably stoic, crying out in pain only a few times as her circulation returned with the help of Macon's skilled hands massaging her frozen flesh. When the pain finally subsided and she was pink and merely chilly, Macon helped her out of the tub and wrapped the towel around her again.

"I'll go get my robe. If I were you, I wouldn't leave those wet underwear on. You can hang them out by the stove. They'll be dry in a few hours."

George was exhausted, and sore all over from the repeated muscle contractions and relentless shivers. She just wanted to lay down. But she peeked around the doorframe and Macon was on the couch, staring into space, his forearms braced on his thighs.

Macon looked over at her and frowned. "What are you doing over there? Come in here. Get warm."

George padded across the floor on the thick wool socks Macon left for her and carefully hung up her lacy bra and underwear on the rope that extended down from the loft rail over the wood burning stove. She curled into the corner of the couch nearest the fire, and furthest from Macon. She stared into the flames through the little glass door on the front of the stove.

He gestured toward the fluorescent pink trainers propped up by the fire. "Those ridiculous shoes are doing a lot of labor. They were like little pink beacons out there. Dunno if I'd have found you, otherwise. *Again*." He sighed in resignation and ran his hands over his face wearily. "What the fuck were you thinking, walking around in this weather, Georgia?"

"Well, it's not like I just decided to take a little jaunt for my health, Macon. My rental broke down. About fifteen miles down the road."

He cursed under this breath. "You're telling me you walked fifteen miles in a blizzard? You should've stayed in the car, sweetheart."

"I'm sorry, Macon."

"What are you sorry for?"

"Coming in hot. Being an asshole, yelling at you." She picked at the robe. "Not telling you the label was dropping you." She looked up. "But it didn't occur to me at the time. It was mentioned in passing and I…" she trailed off. She lifted her hands and finally met his eyes. "No. No excuses. I'm sorry. I wish I could just start over."

"You're going through a lot right now, Peaches." She was relieved to hear him use her nickname. Maybe it meant he wasn't as angry as she was expecting. Maybe he'd even forgive her.

"I handled all of this so poorly, so unprofessionally. You didn't deserve to take the brunt of what's happening in my private life. None of that is your problem. And I didn't mean all the things I said about you."

He thought for a long moment and sighed. "I suppose you were right about some of it. I have used this place as a shield against the world. Can you live with this as a solution? We're square if you can accept my apology for sending in those tracks. It honestly didn't occur to me that it would upset you. I'm sorry I betrayed your trust."

"I'll forget you fucking outed me to my boss. And you'll forget I'm a baby who throws phones in lakes." She made a skeptical face. "I guess."

Macon grinned. "Okay, but it was kinda funny. *Plop*."

"No," she said dryly. "It really wasn't."

He chuckled as he stood and poured cups of coffee for them from the carafe. "Can I ask you something?"

"Sure?"

"Why is it such a big deal for people to know you can sing, or that you're a great producer, or whatever it is that's bothering you about all this? Especially Lucia. I thought she was, like... a big sister to you. Why wouldn't she know that about you already?" He spooned sugar into her cup and stirred.

"I've always been very intentional about the pieces of myself I let people see. I don't like being... perceived."

"That's a shame. I think the whole world should perceive you, Georgia Lane Robinson."

An electric shock hit her square in the heart, and she looked up at him in surprise. He moved across the small space with the mugs in his hand and passed one to her. He perched on the coffee table directly in front of George, and his expression was serious. He was so close, he had to spread his legs wide and bracket her knees with his to fit in the spot.

He handed her the mug and watched as she took a few sips. He took it out of her hands and put it on the table. She looked up at him questioningly.

"I should've told you this before now, Georgia."

She opened her mouth to ask what he meant, but she didn't have a chance, because suddenly Macon's lips were pressed against hers, and his hands were holding her face, his fingertips pushing into her damp hair, and George just about thought she'd die with how good his tongue felt slipping along her parted lips. She angled her chin to deepen the kiss and brought her chilled fingers to his beard. His kiss was as hot, sweet, and dark as the coffee she could still taste on his lips. She dug in and pulled his face closer, and his hands dropped from her face to her neck.

He broke the kiss and lingered at her lips for several seconds before he leaned back. "That's what I needed to say. I'll let you talk now."

"Who wants to talk?" She looked around the room. "Not me." She pulled on his shirt collar, tugging him toward her. He let her draw him in for another kiss, and her whole body was trembling and burning by the time he was done with her. He reached up and gently removed her hands from his shirt.

"I'm trying to be a gentleman, Georgia."

"Oh, fuck no." George shook her head and shot up from the couch. "I'm done trying to come up with answers for this 'will they, won't they' shit. I can't bear it anymore, Macon." *You're begging. Way to go, George.*

He grinned up at her. "Who's asking about that?"

"I am," she answered curtly.

He stood, too, and she found herself face to face with his

chest, being herded toward his room. "We can talk about it in the morning. Come to bed." He gave her a little push and she moved forward.

"To *bed*. With *you*."

"To bed, with me."

"But we're not sleeping together," she continued as she paused in the open door to his room.

"Not tonight," he growled as he pushed her in.

"This is bullshit," she commented, then squealed as he picked her up in his arms again and settled her in the bed, pulling the fluffy duvet around her. He disappeared through the door and the room beyond darkened by degrees as he blew out all the candles, until he returned with the last one in his hand and set it on the bedside table. George watched shyly from the cloud of featherdown comforter piled around her as he stripped off his thermals, down to his boxer briefs. The low light caught all the ripples and planes of his body and illuminated the colorful ink that covered his arms.

He climbed into bed next to her, pulled the comforter up to his chest, and threw his arms behind his head. "Come here." He patted his bicep closest to her, and she hesitantly laid down and rested her head on it, then rolled into him and placed her hand on his hard chest. He was hot under her fingers, and she snuggled into his warmth.

"I'll have you warmed up and thinking clearly by morning," he said quietly. "Hypothermia fucks with your decision-making ability."

"Is that why you're torturing me? Because you think I've gone daft from the cold?"

He laughed softly. "How am I torturing you?"

"Macon." She brought her leg up and threw it over his thigh and she heard him blow a soft stream of air through his pursed lips. "Yeah, this isn't weird at all, right? Just a couple old friends in bed together with no clothes on. Nothing torturous about this."

He chuckled and his arm came down to squeeze her in closer. She loved the feel of all that muscle bracing her, and his skin smelled deliciously of woodsmoke and pine pitch.

"I won't be that guy. I'm trying to make the right decisions while you're dealing with catastrophic, life-changing shit. Times like these, you make bad choices because it feels like everything's on fire, so why the fuck not? I don't wanna be one of your bad decisions. That's the only thing I can control about this situation."

"What in god's name would make you think you need to do that?" She shifted under the covers. "Other than being prone to near death experiences, I'm actually pretty good at taking care of myself," she added lightly.

"You're good at surviving, Georgia. You're not good at taking care of yourself, otherwise you wouldn't be having panic attacks every five seconds."

She changed the subject. "You're not a bad decision, Macon. You're a very real and full human being to me, not some tool I'm using to get through my grief."

"We – as we are here and now – can't exist outside these circumstances. But I exist here. This is my life."

"Why does it have to be something else? Why can't it just be this one night?" She ran her fingers softly over his chest, and she could feel the tremor that ran through him.

"Because then we veer right back into bad choices territory."

"Is this refusal of gratification a kink or something? I don't mean to press, Macon, but it's not like I don't know when someone wants me. I'm not asking for anything from you.

Can't we just make each other feel good?"

"I'll make you feel good, Peaches," he murmured as he twisted on his side to face her. His hand came to her belly and slid down until his fingertips were nearly to the apex of her thighs. She caught his wrist and stopped him.

"I don't want a pity hand job. That's so much more embarrassing than being rejected." Their eyes glittered in the dark in a silent standoff.

He continued his downward trajectory, ignoring her grasp, and cupped his hand over her sex. She gasped as one of his thick fingers moved and pressed into her. He rocked his hand against her and she moaned.

"Pity?" He pressed into her again and watched her in the candlelight as she bit her lip and pushed against his fingers with a soft sigh. "You think I'm not getting anything out of this?"

"What could you…" she gasped. "Possibly." She moaned softly as his fingers moved in her, and then she was wordless and writhing as he worked her. Her hand drifted down to his waistband where she encountered substantial evidence of his enjoyment.

His breath was at her cheek, his voice low and rough. "You think I don't like finding you all hot and wet for me? Baby, you're giving me everything I need right now."

She cried out and clenched hard against his fingers, arching against the pressure of his forearm that pinned her torso.

"The sounds you make." A noise of approval rumbled through his chest as she sighed and groaned. "That's right. Just like that."

He continued to caress her softly until her legs stopped shaking. He lifted his hand to his mouth and licked his fingers clean, one-by-one, his eyes never leaving hers. She moaned as she watched him.

"The way you taste… fuck. No, I'll have my pleasure. Right now, and long after you're gone, Georgia. Night after night." His gaze burned into her.

George's chest heaved, her breath short and erratic.

"But for now, we're going to sleep."

She whined in protest, but he pulled her into his body with an iron grip and shushed her. Her breathing gradually slowed as she melted into his hot skin, and George drifted off to sleep.

When she woke, it was with the back of her neck between Macon's teeth, his hot breath fanning against her. His body enveloped hers from behind. Subdued light filtered through the window as dawn approached, and thick snow fell softly against the deep blue backdrop of the dying night. George made a small noise in her throat and his arm tightened around her. His hand came up to cup her breast, and she exhaled with a small moan. His body was generating an extraordinary amount of heat, but somehow his thick cock, where it pressed against the back of her thigh, was even hotter.

Her pulse beat heavily between her legs. George ground her ass against him, and he growled at her ear. He made a line of kisses from the base of her neck to her hairline, then traced it back with his tongue as she squirmed beneath him. His hand moved down to skate over her clit.

"I'm of sound mind!" She blurted out in a pleading voice. "For god's sake, I consent, or whatever it is you need to hear!"

Macon laughed, low and sexy, at her ear. She made a noise of protest as his heat rolled away from her, and she heard a drawer roll open. A telltale crinkle of metal and plastic, and the slow motions of him moving behind her. Her breath caught and she was thrust into a moment of reality. It had been so long since she'd had sex with anyone other than Kato that she didn't even think about protection. She took a moment to process and decided she hadn't changed her mind just as Macon rolled back into her body.

She had a sudden flash of irrational jealousy for whoever it was Macon had needed those condoms for.

"Get a lotta action out here in the woods?" she asked teasingly.

"That really what you wanna talk about right now, Georgia?" He asked softly as he arranged her body like he wanted it. He threw a leg over hers, keeping her back firmly drawn into his chest, and pressed the length of his cock against her ass. "You wanna bring other people into this bed, or am I enough?"

"You're enough," she whispered.

"Good," he answered into her ear. "Because I'd rather talk about how you kept pushing your perfect ass against my cock all night. I've been hard for you for hours." She whimpered at his words.

He parted her gently and found her dripping for him. He murmured in her ear as he ran his fingers up and down her seam, then lifted her slightly and impaled her on his cock. He slid in slowly and George let out a guttural moan when she'd taken as much of him as she could. She was so filled up, it felt as though he was pressing on every surface inside of her body. He made a V with his fingers around her clit and pressed down as he pushed his hips into her slowly from behind.

George rolled her ass into him again and again, hazy with pleasure. She moaned and sighed as he played with her. He's so fucking good at this. Her mind drifted into a trancelike state as the entire length of his body rubbed her rhythmically from top to bottom.

He thrust into her harder and she groaned loudly. "Where'd you go, Georgia? I'm not doing enough to keep you present?" He sat up and pulled her up with him, her back against his burning hot chest. He threaded his fingers through the hair at the back of her head and pulled her against his body until her neck was gently arched. He ran his lips down the line of her throat, then pushed her forward until she was on her hands and knees. He smacked her ass lightly, his other fist still gripping a handful of her blonde hair.

"Do I have your full attention now, Peach?" He released her hair gently and ran his hands slowly down her back. They slid to her hips in an iron grip and he drove into her, pulling her back roughly as he smashed into her. She cried out with each thrust as heavy pressure began to build in her core.

His hands moved to her ribs, and before she knew what was happening, she was on her back. His body covered every inch of hers and he pushed into her again, grinding deliciously against her clit. He held himself up on one elbow and looked down at her. George dug her fingers into his muscular ass as he rolled his hips against her relentlessly.

"I wanna see your face when you come," he growled.

At that, George's whole body contracted, and that

pounding pressure at her core released like the crack of a whip, bending her spine and leaving her moaning wordlessly as it rushed over her skin and thumped a heavy beat in her belly. He groaned as she tightened and pulsed around him, her clutching walls pulling him in. The muscles in his neck tightened into cords and he uttered a rough growl as he spent. He fell softly to her side and caught her into a spoon position. He whispered sweet things into her ear while he stroked her arms and hair. Eventually they both went back to sleep and didn't wake again until it was nearly noon.

19

Trumspringa

(n.) The longing to wander off your career track in pursuit
of a simple life

"Pretty," she said. On his suspicious look she added, "The Cranberries." Macon leaned back against the headboard with his finger on his chin. George straddled his waist and grinned down at him.

"I could give you three more standalone pretties, but that feels like cheating."

George shrugged. "Up to you how you wanna play the game."

"Pretty Paper." He looked at her with a challenge in his eyes as he reached up and caressed her hip.

"Paper Kites," she answered quickly.

"Can you even do bands?"

"Bands, songs, albums, artists. That's how I always played it."

His eyes narrowed and he shot her an evil grin. "Kites by Geographer. Good luck with that one."

"It's still just 'kites!'" She laughed. She thought for a few seconds. "But I don't know any other kites. Dammit, you won again."

"I remain the champion." He grabbed her around the ribs and she squealed. He pulled her in for a kiss and she spent the next few minutes focused on his mouth. She nuzzled into his neck and inhaled him.

"I'm supposed to be getting on a plane right now," she said into his ear. "But I'm here in bed with you, so who's the champion, really?"

"You're so much less upset about this than I thought you'd be."

"Um, well. I'm going home with nothing but my job, and no one knows or cares where I am, and I haven't been in contact with anyone in – how long have we been trapped here?"

"Six days."

"Six days, then. I'm not upset. I've just abandoned all hope of salvaging my life, so I'm living in the moment."

He grinned. "Are you gonna get in trouble at work?"

"Ironically, the source of my distraction and my salvation are the same. Lucia is crazy about the tracks you sent. And if she really needs to know where I am, I'm sure she can see the weather. She'll figure it out. Right now, no one else really matters or gives a shit."

"We'll be able to get out of here by the end of the week. I'm sure the highways have been clear for days already. I just need a break in this snow to deal with the driveway."

"I'm not in a hurry."

He cocked an eyebrow. "No?"

"Is it wrong to just want a little longer? Like this?"

"We're out of condoms." The corners of his mouth twitched with amusement.

"Well, that's a huge problem. We need to get to town right away."

His eyes crinkled at the corners as he laughed and pulled

her in for another sweet, slow kiss.

Not for the first or last time, George appreciated how finely he'd aged. The smoothly sculpted good looks, clean jaw, and the much leaner form he embodied in his youth had nothing on this fine, thickly muscled, lined and scarred, silver-touched, grown-ass man.

George stood at the kitchen counter, mixing cornbread from a box in a large bowl. Macon's flannel went to her knees. She stopped to roll up the sleeves a little further, so she didn't get any food on them. She ran a whisk through the batter, lost in thoughts of what it would be like to exist with him as a long-term situation. It was a silly, unrealistic pipe dream, but she couldn't help fantasizing about waking up to him every day. Playing wifey, playing house. The thought made her heart thump like a kick drum.

The door opened, and Macon finally stomped into the cabin. He stood by the stove thawing out his icy beard and watching the flames. "I cleared the driveway," he said quietly.

"Oh," she said, trying to feign cheer. "That's great. Thank you."

"I'll drive you into the city tomorrow so you can pick up a new phone. Deal with the rental. All that shit."

"That means I might have two more days, max, before I have to head back." She sighed heavily.

"Yeah," he said. He moved across the room and pulled her into his arms. "Maybe we don't have to think about that right now."

She looked up at him as he leaned in and found her lips, and for a time, she didn't think about anything other than his mouth all over her body. She forgot the meal she was making altogether as his shirt puddled around her feet.

Sunlight streamed through the small window. Shatters of light coming through the heavy icicles along the gutters shifted on the walls. Melting, dripping water was the only sound other than the wet noise of what Macon was doing to her with his tongue, and her soft, answering gasps and sighs. She arched into the pillows and cried out softly.

Macon was making progress back up her body with his lips when he stopped abruptly and sat up, his salt and pepper streaks wild where her fingers had been gripping them just seconds prior.

"Someone's here," he muttered. He struggled out of the tangled covers and hopped out of bed, pulled on his boxer briefs, and swung his robe over his shoulders just as the sound of tires crunching against gravel sounded outside. A car door slammed.

He moved quickly into the front room as the stomp of feet on the wood decking approached the door. The person on the other side pounded on the heavy wood surface with the sharp impact of a cop-knock, and in the bedroom, George sat up in alarm.

Macon threw open the door. "Can I *help you*?" he asked acerbically. The woman scowling before him hardly looked at his face before she pushed him aside and moved into the house to his expression of disbelief.

"Where the fuck is she?"

"Who?" he asked, mystified.

"Oh, goddammit, Macon. You know who."

Understanding registered on his face, and his expression rapidly changed from annoyance and incredulity to panic.

Then Lucia was standing in the doorway of the bedroom, taking in Georgia's disheveled hair, wide eyes, and the hand she held against her chest, protectively clutching a sheet against her nakedness. Lucia's back straightened, and her lips flattened. She shook her head, displeasure radiating from every inch of her tight body. "Oh, my god," she muttered in exasperation. "So, this is it?"

"What?" George whispered.

"After a week no-contact, *this* is your grand implosion? You'd throw it all away for *that*?" She gestured back at Macon, who was standing slightly behind her wearing a sheepish expression, his robe open at the front. She paused to take him in, and her face softened as she spared some appreciation for his form. "I guess if you're gonna throw it all away..." She shrugged, then looked back at George with a glare. "I'm calling an end to your midlife crisis. Get dressed," she bit, "I'm taking you home."

George leaned in to change the music playing on the car stereo and Lucia slapped her hand away. "Leave it," she clipped. "No more sad songs for you, sad girl. What the fuck happened back there?" She sighed. "I didn't expect this kind of behavior from you."

"I don't know." George leaned back and stared silently out the window. After a long moment, she shrugged and turned slightly to see Lucia's eyes just sliding back to the road. "We have history," George mumbled.

"Apparently." They sped along in silence. "I'm not letting you throw away your dreams just for some good dick, Georgia."

George made an indignant noise of protest next to her.

"Oh, come on, George. Kato's as gay as the day is long. No way you were getting fucked right in that relationship. You have no idea how many discussions Sharon and I have had about you two. No one's fooled."

George gasped. "Kato's not gay," she said defensively. "He's… bi. I guess. Or something. We were having sex." Lucia shot her a skeptical look. "This is so inappropriate. Why are we all talking about my sex life, anyway?" She scowled and slumped into her seat.

"Because you were clearly in need of whatever that big lumberjack of a man-chunk back there was giving you. I'm not fucking stupid, George. This is the first time I've seen you in two years that your shoulders haven't been attached to your earlobes. I'm telling you, it's not worth it."

"I can't believe you came all the way out here," George finally mumbled, and Lucia made an irritated noise in her throat.

"Sharon made me," Lucia answered. "So, you have my wife to thank for saving your career. You should call her when we get back. Send her a fruit basket or some shit. And you owe me."

Georgia made a non-committal noise in her chest and looked out the window. All she could think about was how Macon wouldn't let go of her hand as she tried to walk away, and the look in his eyes when she shut the car door between them.

She had a life to get back to.

She was never going to be able to stay here.

Lucia was right, of course. As she usually was in practical matters.

She tried her best to hold back the tears that welled up in

her eyes, and the sadness that weighed her heart down more with every mile of road the car ate up. She rationalized her feelings. She was fixating on Macon. He was a life raft. This wasn't love; she'd barely known this iteration of him for a month-and-a-half. And if it wasn't love, it wasn't worth the distraction. She should fixate on work and getting her messy life cleaned up, instead. That was the way through this: control and focus.

Eventually her tears spilled over, and she cried in earnest until she was all dried up and empty.

Beloiter

(v. intr.) To look around in a state of mild astonishment that your life is somehow still going, as if a part of you had just assumed that your allotment of days would've been used up by now.

George tapped out an email and turned up the volume on her speakers as she straightened a pile of contracts on her desk.

"*I lost myself for you, now there's nothing left of me. I don't want you to apologize, I want you outta my head, I want you outta my head…*" she mumbled along with the music.

Lucia tapped on the door and stuck her head in. "For god's sake, George. Are you still listening to that breakup playlist? It's been almost six months. We need to get you out of your head. Come out with Sharon and me tonight. There's someone I want you to meet."

George leveled her with a flat look. "Who?"

"A new friend of ours. A performer."

"Oh, got it." She relaxed. "This is talent. I thought we were talking about a dating type thing. What time?"

Lucia eyed her. "Seven, Little Door." She started to close the door and leaned in again. "And I mean it, enough with these playlists. If I have to hear that Thomas Day song one more time, I'll strangle you with my scarf. And no more fucking Mitski, for the love of all that's holy. Also, sorry to bring up a verboten topic, but have you seen your lumberjack's numbers yet?"

"I know. He's charting." George took a deep breath and looked down at the papers on her desk.

"You'll pull a significant bonus off those producer and performer points. We're offering him a contract renewal."

"Great," George said flatly.

Lucia pursed her lips and shook her head before disappearing back into the hall. George waited until she was out of sight before she opened a folder on her computer. Her mouse hovered over a file, and she hesitated. Macon wouldn't let her play the track during their whirlwind week beneath the sheets. By the time the single dropped, George refused to listen to it. There was no way it wasn't about her. But he was charting. She held her breath. Listening to a song written about her while still pining for its writer was tantamount to drunk-dialing an ex. Less embarrassing, maybe. But just as stupid and reckless. She hovered for a second more, then clicked. She managed to keep a straight face until the first chorus.

You're reckless, you're restless
Too far from home
I'll be the calm at the eye of it all
You're breathless, your heart breaks
But I am a stone
I can be the shore that you break on

You, the storm, are caught in
This old dance and song

The harbor I could offer in these arms
If you ever thought to come home

But you live for the tempest
And I live alone

She closed her eyes and a sob caught in her throat. She hadn't listened to any of the finished album. She couldn't bear hearing his voice and remembering the warmth of his knee against hers as they perched on milk crates in the small recording room.

"Get it together, George," she muttered aloud. She dabbed the tears welling up in her eyes with the cuff of her sweater. She turned the camera to selfie mode and made sure her eyeliner wasn't messed up. The cat eye was perfect. She experienced a brief moment of satisfaction in her skillful crying technique.

She looked down at the bulky sweater, black leggings, and boots combo she was wearing and sighed. It wasn't the best look for a meeting with new talent, but she didn't have time to go home and get back to the restaurant in time. She fixed her lipstick and let her long, layered locks fall from the clip holding them up. It would have to do.

The patio was strung with thousands of twinkle lights, and little gold lanterns that hung on looping strands from the leafy canopy above. The hostess seated her at a table in the corner.

Lucia wove her way through the restaurant and George waved. She approached the table quickly and looked around. "I'm so sorry, George, but something important came up.

Sharon and I can't stay." She handed her a sealed manila envelope. "Give this to him when he gets here. I'll call you later, hm? Enjoy the night."

Him? George just assumed that, because Sharon and Lucia hung with a lesbian-heavy crowd, a new friend meant a woman. And now she was going to have to entertain some dude on her own. *Ugh. I hope he's queer, at least.* She was engrossed in studying the twinkle lights above when a deep voice came from her side, and she jumped out of her chair so quickly, she almost knocked over her water glass.

Macon stood before her, with hardly enough hair on his cheeks to be called a beard, a fresh haircut, and a fashionable shirt with a deep cut in the neckline that showed off his chest. George's heart surged, but she was frozen in place. She couldn't believe he was really standing right in front of her, looking insanely hot and unfamiliar in his city clothes. His eyes searched her face for a moment, but his face remained impassive. He moved to the chair across from her and dropped into it.

"This is not the meeting I thought I was attending."

"Yeah," she said breathlessly. "Big surprise to me, too."

"How've you been, George?"

Horrible. Despondent. Dead inside. "I'm alright," she answered. "You?"

"Great."

"That's… great," she said lamely. "Oh, uh… I'm supposed to give you this. It's from Lucia." She slid the envelope across the table to him. "Something came up and they couldn't make it."

He shot her an exasperated look. "Yeah, so she said. I'm sure this was all a complete accident."

"What do you mean?" George was glad it was dark, because she could feel a furious rush of heat rising on her cheeks.

He sighed and leaned forward, with his elbows on the table. "Listen, Lucia made more than one allusion to your state of mind. She seems to think I can do something about it. I feel a little ambushed right now, to be completely honest." He leaned back, crossed his arms, and looked out at the restaurant. "I don't know what the hell we're doing here."

Inside, what little remained of her heart crumpled to dust. Pain rippled through her chest, and her lungs couldn't seem to fill up. "I'm so sorry. I hope you know I had nothing to do with this." She could hardly speak above a whisper. "Excuse me." She stood quickly and fled to the bathroom.

She leaned against the wall of the bathroom stall, looking up at the ceiling and trying not to let the tears spill out of her eyes as she gasped for breath. She swallowed heavily several times and forced herself to breathe deeply until she had control of herself. She'd lingered too long; it had to have been ten minutes, at least, since she left the table. She sniffled, blew her nose, and squared her shoulders. When she exited the bathroom, however, she couldn't bring herself to go back to the table. She thought she might drop dead right there if she had to look at his aloof face for one more second. She closed her eyes and dropped her chin as she leaned against the white plaster wall in a concealing swag of live vines growing from a planter.

Her eyes popped open as she heard footsteps approach. In her sudden, surprised scramble to flee from Macon as he neared, she moved backward into the planter she was using as cover and lost her footing. She went careening onto the tile floor and, such as it was, the best option she could think of was to continue lying face down on the ground. She might as well be lying down if she was about to melt through the floor and die anyway.

Macon rushed to her and peeled her off the cold tile, then helped her stand. "Jesus, are you alright?" He frowned as he looked her over. "All in one piece? Nothing broken?"

Honestly, nothing is broken except for my heart. "I'm okay."

He moved closer to her, and she shied away from him into the wall. "Where you going, George?" He reached for her.

"Don't touch me," she gasped.

He stepped back slightly and his frown deepened. "What's going on with you?"

"You cannot just come here and put your hands on me."

"I was helping you up, George, what the fuck. Should I have left you lying on the floor like a dead animal?"

"You just… I can't…" She went to her knees in the small hallway and covered her face with her hands as sobs shook her body. "I can't be this close to you," she wept.

"Shit, Georgia. Come on. *Shh.* Come on, get up. Let's get out of here." He took her arm and she ripped it free.

"Please, Macon," she whispered up to him. Mascara streaked her face.

A perfectly coiffed, white-haired, older woman squeezed past them. She eyed George with concern, then shot a hateful glare in Macon's direction and shook her head in disgust before she entered the bathroom.

He knelt down. "Come on, Georgia. *Please.*" He gently took her arm and pulled her to her feet. "Fuck. Stay here. I'll be right back."

George leaned back against the wall and tried to stop

crying, but the dam had cracked and there wasn't anything she could do to stop the flood of tears. Macon disappeared in the direction of the patio just as the woman exited the bathroom and put a light hand on George's shoulder.

"Are you okay, sweetheart? Do you need help?" she asked with kind concern.

"No, thank you so much," George sniffled and forced a smile. "I'm just having a hell of a… a year," she finished wryly. "Sorry."

The woman nodded understandingly. "No apology needed. I just wanted to make sure you were safe before I left. He…didn't…?" she looked in the direction of the restaurant and raised her eyebrows.

"Oh, god no. He's the only normal one here," she said dryly. "He didn't do anything to me. I'm afraid it's exclusively my fault a scene was made." She sniffed and wiped her eyes.

The woman's face broke into a soft, sympathetic smile. "You're fine, sweetie. We all deserve a little meltdown here and again. Just as a treat." George burst into unexpected laughter through her waning tears. The woman winked and patted her arm. "Take care, honey."

"Thank you," George whispered as the woman departed.

George was holding it together by the time Macon came back to fetch her, with her purse in one hand and the manila envelope in the other. She allowed him to take her arm and lead her out to the street.

They strolled down Sunset wordlessly, her purse slung over Macon's shoulder. Macon sat down on a retaining wall in front of a dark office building and patted the spot next to him. George looked at the wall for a moment, then sat.

He looked at her sideways and cocked an eyebrow.

"What?" George pushed the toe of her boot along a crack in the sidewalk.

"You gonna tell me what's going on, or do I have to dig it out of you?"

"Nothing's going on." She stared at the traffic on the boulevard.

"You were literally lying face down on the floor of a restaurant ten minutes ago."

"I was catching my breath."

Macon bit his lip to keep from laughing even as annoyance flashed over his face at her flippant answer. He frowned in concern. "When I picked you up, you felt like a feather."

She shrugged. "People lose weight, Macon. It's not the end of the world."

"Where's your house?"

"I don't want you to know."

"God-fucking-dammit, Georgia!"

"I'll call an Uber and be out of your hair momentarily. You can do whatever it is you thought you'd be doing tonight." She swatted him away as she opened the app. Macon leaned in and snatched the phone out of her fingers, and George reached for it with an indignant screech. He repelled her easily with one arm.

He handed it back after tapping on it for a few seconds. She looked at the destination address and frowned. "What's this? This isn't my house."

He rolled his eyes. "It's my hotel. I was gonna help you get home, but you decided to be difficult. And we need to go somewhere we can discuss this. I'm supposed to leave it with you if I decide to sign it." He hefted the thick envelope.

"I don't even know what that is. Lucia gave it to me before she bailed."

"It's my contract."

"What's to discuss? You either sign or you don't." She lifted her hands and let them fall to her sides. "I have nothing to do with legal. I can't approve any changes."

Macon's lips tightened and he shook his head. "I'm only here for the night, George. This can't wait. Okay? I know you don't want to be anywhere near me, but we just need to get through some business. Can you be bothered? I thought work was the most important thing to you?"

George sniffed and stood up. "Absolutely, it is. Let's go." She stared straight ahead into the street until the car arrived. She got into the back seat with him and looked out the window in silence until they reached The Ritz.

"I have a suite," he said as they exited the car and made their way for the entrance. "It's big and quiet, and there's a sitting area where we can talk."

"Fine, Macon. Let's just do what we need to do so I can go home."

As they rode the elevator up, feet apart and silent, George swayed on her feet, and before she knew what was happening, she was opening her eyes and Macon was hauling her up by her armpits.

"Did I pass out?" A deep frown creased George's face.

"Fuck, Georgia." Macon grasped the sides of her torso as he held her steady. His face was pale, and he wore an uncharacteristic expression of alarm. "Baby."

George shook her head and wriggled from his grasp. "Don't call me baby," she clipped. "I'm not your baby. Do you only want me when I need to be rescued? Is that it? You couldn't fucking bear to be nice to me at the restaurant but now that Georgie's all fucked up, I'm your baby?"

His jaw tensed. "I swear to fuckin' Christ, Georgia. You are going to drive me to the very brink of madness, aren't you?"

She looked up at him wearily. "Welcome to the club."

He took in her hollow cheeks and eyes, the dark smudges, her blocky movements. He waited until they were in his room before he brought it up. "I think we have more to talk about than business. When was the last time you ate?"

She glowered at him. "You don't have to worry about that, Macon. You're not my caretaker. I'm a representative of your label. That's all. You made that super clear when you didn't get in touch for five months."

"Lucia told me in no uncertain terms to leave you the fuck alone."

"And you listened to her?" George made a skeptical face.

"Need I remind you that you went with her willingly?"

"I had a whole fucking life to get back to, Macon!" she cried. "I have a job. A mortgage. And Lucia looks out for me. She always has. What the hell was I supposed to do? If I lost this job, I'd have *nothing.*"

"She told me I was a distraction. That I'd keep you from healing."

George covered her mouth and swayed on her feet again. She felt sick that Lucia would have done something like that when the evidence of her pain was so clear. She found herself tipping, then caught in Macon's grip again as she made an irritated noise. "I'm really tired. That's all."

Macon leveled her in a stare. "When was the last time you

ate?" he asked again.

"I dunno," she mumbled. "Probably lunch." But she thought back and realized she hadn't eaten lunch, or breakfast, or even dinner the night before. Macon stepped into her before she could protest and pulled her close. She shivered as he pushed his hand under the edge of her sweater and ran it up one side of her back. He sighed. "You're skin and bones, Georgia." He led her gently to the couch and prodded her until she sat, then disappeared into the other half of his suite, where she could hear his muffled voice. She hated herself, that she was so hungry for his touch. He reappeared with a glass of water in his hand and put it in front of her.

"Have some of that. Food'll be up shortly." He sat down close to her and braced his arms on his legs. They sat in silence for several long minutes. He pushed the glass of water toward her. "Drink. I haven't been at the cabin for a while."

"Well. You've been on tour, I guess." Her lips were numb, but it was easier to fall into small talk than to let the heavy silence persist. She picked up the water and took a sip.

"Yeah, just picked up in February. I've been on the road for two months already."

"Hope it's going great."

"Shows are sold out. But I gotta be honest. I'm not loving it."

"No?" She finally broke her thousand-yard stare and turned to look at him. "Always seemed like you loved the stage."

"I do. But it just makes me feel my age now. I'd rather be somewhere quiet." He bumped his knee against hers. "I'd rather be coming in from chopping firewood to find you in my kitchen making cornbread." He looked down at her and George hung her head.

"Please don't mess with me, Macon. It's not fair. Leaving you broke me." She gestured at herself. "And that's probably something I should be worried about, right? Like, I'm not supposed to let myself die because some guy I hardly know doesn't want me. I'm acting like a fool and I know it. I see it, trust me. I just can't make it stop."

"You were the one who left."

"*I* control who has access to my time," she said in a mocking tone. "*You* said that. How the hell was I supposed to get in touch with no way to do so, and an edict like that hanging over me?"

A knock at the door startled them both and Macon leapt up to receive the room service. He tipped the porter and waved him off, then rolled the cart close to the couch. "I got a little of everything. I don't know what you eat when you're not stuck in the woods with a canned-stew-eating Neanderthal."

"I'm not picky." She already knew by his tone that he was going to make her eat something, and she was too worn out to argue.

He peeked under several of the cloches and pulled out a bread roll, a small cut of chicken. He cut off a few bites of a cheeseburger. She watched him add small pieces of everything to the plate he was building.

"Did you order any vegetables?" The corners of her mouth twitched in amusement.

"I was more focused on high-calorie stuff." He handed her the finished plate with a pointed look. "I know what you're supposed to feel like under that tent you're wearing, Georgia. Did you forget that I know you intimately? Eat."

Her face reddened as she took a tentative bite of chicken. "Of course, I didn't forget." *It's all I've been thinking of for the last five months.*

"I'm pretty well acquainted with your body, and I know I shouldn't be able to feel your fucking spine." He looked angry.

She looked away and changed the subject. "What the fuck am I supposed to do with that little cornbread and firewood anecdote, anyway? You want me to leave my job behind and come live in a cabin in the woods with you?" Imagining it sent a stab of pain through her sternum, and she clutched her chest absently. His eyes fell to her hand over her heart and the lines between his eyebrows deepened. "Or do you wanna come live in my condo in midtown? I know how much you love LA."

"I didn't say there was an easy solution," he answered quietly.

George stopped chewing and looked at her toes. She forced herself to swallow the food that was sitting like sawdust on her tongue. "I've never let anyone hurt me like this, Macon. I've learned my lesson. I won't do it again."

Macon moved closer to her and wordlessly pulled her into his lap. George pushed against the couch and struggled against his grasp, but she was too tired, too weak to resist for very long and eventually she collapsed against him. It wasn't until he wrapped his warm arms around her thin frame that she realized how cold she was. How cold she'd been for months. Colder than she ever was when she wandered through a blizzard in the Upper Peninsula. His heat seeped into her as she rested her head against his chest. For the first time in months, simply breathing in and out didn't feel like a struggle.

He leaned forward and snagged the bread from the plate. He tore off a small piece and touched it to her lips. "Eat." She obediently took it between her teeth and chewed. A small piece of chicken. "Eat." Butter-seared scallop. "Eat." Burrata and peach. "Eat." Until the plate was half-empty, and she turned her head aside.

"Sorry. I'm trying, but this is more than I've eaten in the past week," she muttered. "I'm so full." Even though she'd only just finished eating, she already felt a surge of well-being prickle over her skin.

"That's okay. You did good, baby." He pulled her back against his chest and rested his chin on her shoulder, so his mouth was at her ear. "Why are you so certain I'm going to hurt you?"

"Because you already did."

"George, I thought it's what you wanted. I thought you were trying to get through this time, and you didn't need the pull of having some kind of fucked up, long-distance relationship with a man with no phone. What do I have to offer? A life of total seclusion in a place you hate? It didn't seem fair."

"That wasn't your decision to make for me."

"That's true," he conceded. "And you're not willing to overlook my mistake? I don't get any more chances?" He squeezed her and she sighed.

"I don't know if I can. It's terrifying where my head has gone these last few months. Seeing how fucked up you've got me after being with you for a total of six weeks… I can't imagine the fallout after six months. Six years. I haven't been good to myself."

"After you left, I considered making some bad decisions of my own. I really thought I'd just slip right off the wagon for a minute."

Her eyes narrowed. "What happened?"

"Old friend showed up at my door with a bottle of wine. It took me getting all the way to the kitchen cabinet and pulling out a single glass before I knew what the answer was."

"Oh," she said flatly. "An old friend."

He chuckled and kissed the back of her ear. "You're so jealous, Peaches. Yes, my eighty-year-old, widowed neighbor, Susie."

"I am jealous. The way I need you is too… overwhelming. Maybe I'm not strong enough to have romantic relationships, you know? Like, that's the concession I need to make so I can be healthy."

"I don't think that's true." He pushed his face into her neck and breathed her in. "I think you're scared because so many people you've loved have died. You think everyone's gonna leave you."

"What if you do, though? What if you leave and I don't live through it? I've been in such a dark place, Macon."

"Are you medicated?" he asked softly. He stroked her hair, letting the ash blonde locks fall through his fingers.

"No. My therapist said the only thing wrong with me is basic clinical depression. She won't recommend medication of any kind. She told me to work out." Georgia paused. "I've been running about twenty-five miles a week, but I can't outrun you. She said I had to give it time."

"Baby, the first thing we need to do is get you a new

therapist."

She snuggled into his chest, and he kissed her ear again.

"I have to be in Phoenix tomorrow. We're pulling out early."

"I can't be a tour widow, Macon. Nothing about this works. Every major factor in our lives is against this happening."

"We'll figure it out," he whispered. "Stop talking, Georgia."

She took a breath as if to say something else, so he twisted her in his lap, took her jaw in hard fingers, and covered her mouth with his. She uttered a single, broken sob against his lips. He nibbled her mouth as he broke the kiss. He touched her face with his lips and soft breath.

"Take a nap," he whispered. "I have you." He adjusted her in his arms until she was curled against his chest. She closed her eyes with a weary sigh. He ran light hands over her hair and limbs until she began to snore softly.

21

Attriage

(n.) The state of having lost all control over how you feel
about someone— not even trying to quench the flames
anymore but lighting other fires around your head just
hoping to contain the damage.

When George woke, Macon was already gone. The
contract folder was on the table in front of her, along
with a plate covered with a cloche. A hotel comment card
was folded into a triangle tent card. A handwritten arrow
pointing to the envelope was labeled "Signed." Another
arrow pointed to the covered plate accompanied by the text,
"Eat."

George smirked at the note, then lifted the cloche to find a
bowl full of berries with a ramekin of whipped cream. She
hefted the folder in her hand and pulled out the thick sheath
of papers. She absently ate berries as she flipped through
the paperwork. She did a double take as her name caught
her eye, nestled in the center of a dense block of text. Her
eyes widened.

"What does this even mean?" she muttered. She ran her
fingers over the text and frowned. "What the fuck?" She read
further and her frown deepened. "What kind of contract is
this?!"

She looked at her phone. It was only 7:30AM on Saturday,

but it couldn't wait. She dialed Lucia and cursed softly when the call went straight to voicemail. She never had her phone off. Georgia got up, used the shower and caught an Uber back to her condo.

She stood in the middle of her living room with her keys in her hand and wrinkled her nose. It was badly in need of a deep cleaning. She took a deep breath as she surveyed the situation. What had she been doing all these months? They'd escaped her so easily. With no Kato and no cat, the nights here ran one into the next. She ran her hand over her face as it sunk in, how long she'd been languishing. In all her life, she'd never allowed herself to break down and lose control quite like this. It frightened her. Something big had to break under so much pressure. If she wasn't more careful, she could see a future where that thing was always her.

Maybe it was finally getting to touch Macon again, or maybe it was the nourishment, but George felt the dark veil of depression begin to lift. She threw her keys on the table and stalked into the kitchen to find the broom.

Three hours later, she was sweaty, streaked with dust, and starving. She plopped down on the couch and ordered in, then tried Lucia again. Straight to voicemail. She pulled up her music app and looked through her playlists. There was still cleaning to be done until she would try Lucia again. She threw on the one that started with *Pink Pony Club.* When her noodles finally arrived, she was spinning through the living room, singing into a hairbrush, and doing a terrible job of finishing the laundry she'd started to fold. It felt good to move. It felt good to clean Kato from the space. She fell into the couch and slurped on ramen from the waxed paper takeout container.

When her apartment was spotless, she tried Lucia. She made a disgusted noise when it went to voicemail again. This was unprecedented behavior. George realized it might be time to worry. She tried Sharon, but her call went to voicemail after a few rings. She tried Misha to see if she knew where they were, but her call went to voicemail, too. The office PA, Blake. Voicemail. *What the fuck?*

George took the rest of the weekend to get her life back in order, and her colleagues continued letting her calls go to voicemail. On Sunday morning, she threw the phone on the charger in her room and decided to ignore it. Not because it was a healthy choice, but out of spite for anyone who might call her back after leaving her hanging all weekend. She walked to the Russian market and stocked up on groceries, and her fridge finally had some color after months of being empty and white, with just a sad contingent of condiments holding down the fort.

She showered, made herself a stir fry, arranged the cut flowers she picked up at the store, and lit a candle. It didn't feel so desolate when it was clean. She wandered the condo. It felt strangely spacious with all of Kato's things gone. She wasn't sure if she wanted to fully reclaim this space. When she got to the bathroom, she tentatively stepped on her bathroom scale. She winced and hissed through her teeth as she saw her weight. Almost forty pounds in five months. She didn't realize it was that bad. Not catastrophic, but not healthy, considering it was practically starvation-induced. *No wonder Macon was freaked out,* she thought. She took off her clothes and stood in front of the full-length mirror in her bedroom examining the softly jutting bones at her hips and along her ribs and collarbone.

"Shit," she muttered. Maybe he was right about that therapist.

She threw on a robe and collapsed into her lounge chair with a fizzy water and a book. After a few pages, she tossed the book on the side table next to her and stared at the candle flame. One of the things she remembered in Michigan was how good it felt to let her mind wander. How it opened up all the best parts of herself so the universe could flow through her. It was where the music came from, and she hadn't been back to that place in a long time.

She suddenly wondered where her guitar was, and remembered it was shoved far back in the wilderness of the crawl space. She climbed the rickety stairs and picked her way past disorganized piles of boxes until she found it. She used an old t-shirt hanging from an open box to clean the thick layer of dust off the case. She wrestled it down before folding the stairs back up into the ceiling.

She sat on the couch and tuned the half-dead strings as best she could. Her fingers hovered over them before she began to pick out a tune. Her fingertips were tender, but they remembered the notes. She hummed and played until the strings made deep, bruised grooves in her flesh before she let the music fade into the quiet evening.

22

Tarrion

(n.) An odd interval of blankness you feel after something big happens to you but before you feel the resulting emotional reaction. The tension-filled seconds between a flash of lightning and the thunderclap that follows, which gives you a hint of how near you are to the coming storm.

George grimaced as she looked at her reflection. The red power dress was too big. Everything was too big. She wasn't about to walk into that office looking under-dressed on this day, but there was nothing in her closet that fit right anymore. She pulled a thin, cashmere off-the-shoulder sweater from the back of the closet and paired it with black leggings and a pair of heels. The dependable power of a good red lipstick would have to do. She examined her face in the mirror and was pleased to see some color returned. After a weekend of sleep and regular food, the dark smudges under her eyes were faded enough for the concealer to do its job reasonably well. She grabbed her keys. She'd be egregiously early, but she couldn't stand to wait around at home.

She held her breath as the elevator slowed. The doors slid open and she was relieved to see the office was still empty. She put on coffee, then flipped on a couple lights and settled at her desk. She was catching up on email when she heard the elevator doors. She craned her neck to see who it was. Blake came around the corner and shot her a little salute through the office window.

Each time the elevator opened, George lifted out of her seat to see who was arriving, and at long last, Lucia stepped into the hall. She immediately locked eyes with George when she rounded the corner and beckoned her to follow as she headed into her office. George shot up out of her chair and scrambled into the hall with Macon's contract in her hand.

Lucia was just settling into her desk when George entered and tossed the papers on the desk. "How was your weekend?" Lucia asked. She ran appraising eyes over George.

"It was a disaster," answered George. "And I think we're square, on that interpersonal debt I accrued when you had to retrieve me," she said breathlessly. "I messed up big time. But so did you. Lucia… how could you do this to me?"

"I miscalculated, babe. I didn't understand how serious it was for you. I was worried about you, genuinely. I'm still worried."

"I haven't been okay. Like, at all."

"I know. I figured that out pretty quickly. I have to tell you, babe, after spending so much time with him, I really do get it. He's a great guy."

"What were you doing spending 'so much time' with Macon?" George frowned.

"Sharon and I were negotiating this contact with him."

"Yeah, okay, about that…"

"Mmm, I thought you'd have questions," Lucia interrupted in a mild tone.

"I sure do." George pointed at the papers. "I'm no lawyer, but it does read as though this contract acceptance is conditional upon my termination. And it alludes to another contract that I don't have any knowledge of. So, I don't entirely understand what I'm reading, but it's not inspiring confidence."

"Why don't you sit down, George? This is probably going to take a while. Coffee?"

George nodded and sat with a bewildered expression.

"Blake!" Lucia shouted and the young man appeared as if by magic in the doorway. "Coffee for Georgia and myself, please. Ah, and bring in some of those lemon muffins from the bakery." Blake disappeared as quickly as he arrived. "Macon told me I had to make sure you had something to eat this morning," Lucia said with an amused expression.

"Oh my god, what a control freak," George muttered. She looked up at Lucia. "I'm dying to know what you and Macon have been negotiating that requires this level of secrecy. What's in this supplemental contract?"

Lucia reached into her desk and pulled out another folder. She pushed it across the desk and George opened it. She read in silence for several minutes before she looked up at Lucia with disbelief in her wide eyes. "Is this real? How... what does this mean for... for my life?"

"Do you have any questions that aren't existential? Like about the conditions outlined in the supplemental? You can take it home and review it at your leisure. Talk to a lawyer."

"So, I just... go back to work, and..." George stammered. "I don't..."

Lucia rose and came around to perch near George on the front of the desk. "Babe, I love you. But this is ultimately my decision. And while you obviously don't have to take this deal, I don't see why you wouldn't. Weber is prepared to invest generously in the project. But your bonus and your severance packages are generous, too. Even if you decide not to do it, you'll be taken care of indefinitely while you figure out what you want to do next."

"That's it? I'm fired?" George's mouth dropped open.

Lucia smiled softly. "It's been my great pleasure to work with you, my dear. You were such an integral part of making this label what it is today. I'll never find another you. But… babes, look at you. This isn't healthy. It hasn't been for a long time. Consider this an intervention, orchestrated by people who care for you madly. This is Sharon, Macon, and me loving you the best way we know how."

George leaned back in her chair and exhaled heavily. "You're firing me." She couldn't wrap her head around what was happening.

"I feel wildly corny saying this like I'm a B-character in a rom-com, but you should go to him. He's headed to SLC today, and he'll be in Denver by this Thursday. There's an all-access pass to the Denver show in your termination paperwork. Go take care of that with HR and we can wrap up anything we don't get to when you're back."

George stood, still in shock, and walked slowly from Lucia's office with both contracts clutched loosely in her hand. She gathered up a few things from her office and made her way to HR in a daze.

When she was done, she stood in front of the iconic Weber Records building and looked up at it. She'd let herself go so badly, the people who cared about her had to blow up her entire life to save her from herself. She shook her head, still stunned by what was happening, even as a tiny, delicious thrill of freedom fluttered over her skin. She loved the job.

It made up the entirety of her thirties, and half her forties.

But maybe she'd been caught in it as surely as she was entangled with Kato in a relationship that felt impossible to extricate from every part of her life. Yet, when Kato decided for her that it was over, it was all wrapped up so neatly and quickly that the lack of messiness, itself, was what made her most sad. Like it was inconsequential that she was ever involved. Maybe it would be like that here, as if she'd never existed.

But Macon and Lucia already orchestrated her breakup from this fraught relationship. And, she realized, she was so fucking relieved that she wasn't even really mad. After all, if she decided to take what they were offering, it wouldn't be at all like stepping into the unknown. It was familiar territory, almost all within her areas of expertise. It sure wasn't getting on a Greyhound from Indy to LA with a single backpack, a guitar, a carton of cigarettes, and no idea where she was landing. It was just… something new. She took a deep breath and walked away from the building that had been her second home for almost twenty years.

Aftersome

(adj.) Astonished to think back on the bizarre sequence of accidents that brought you to where you are today—as if you'd spent years passing through a million harmless decision points, any one of which might've changed everything—which makes your long and winding path feel fated from the start, yet so unlikely as to be virtually impossible.

Macon stood before the mic and raised his hand to shield his eyes from the bright stage lights. "Lotta high end in the left monitor, buddy," he said into the mic.

The sound guy's voice came through the monitors. "Gotcha. Can you turn that second mic on so we can test the backup singer's levels?"

"They're late," Macon said with an annoyed expression. "But I'll hop on it for now. I'll want a quick level-set with all of us."

"Okay, let's get those vox with the uh… are you gonna use that second acoustic guitar?"

"Yeah, for sure." Macon picked up the second guitar and moved to the extra mic. He started strumming aimlessly.

"Play something for a minute, I'm having some board issues up here I wanna work out before the openers do their checks."

"No problem," Macon said into the mic. He stepped back

and played the opening notes of You, the Storm. He stepped into the microphone, and his voice filled the mostly empty venue.

You're reckless, you're restless
Too far from home

From the main mic, a second voice joined.

I'll be the calm at the eye of it all

George's sweet, husky alto lifted the harmony into the rafters and Macon turned in surprise. After a moment, he continued to strum, and George finished the song with him.

They stood, locked in an intense stare until the sound guy's voice broke into their moment. "Hey, can I get you guys to switch up on those mics?"

Macon looked up in surprise, like he was just remembering he and George weren't the only two people in the auditorium. "I'm gonna take a minute. We're good, yeah?"

"Yeah, man. I can tweak it later." The sound guy gave him a little wave.

Macon carefully placed his guitar in the stand and turned to her slowly, as if he still couldn't believe she was there. He took her hand and led her offstage. As soon as they were in the all-black, backstage hallway beyond, he grabbed her up, swung her into his arms, and kissed her soundly before setting her lightly on her feet.

"You look good, Peaches. Your color is back." He ran his fingers down her jawline. "You've been eating."

"It's only been a week," she said with a small smile.

"Still. What are you doing here?" His eyes were dark, blue pools of need as they ran over her. His hands touched her arms lightly, and he found himself unable to break physical contact with her.

"Somebody got me fired." She cocked an eyebrow at him.

He ran his hand over the back of his neck and wrinkled his nose. "You mad?"

"Why would I be?" she asked lightly. "I love it when people make life-changing decisions on my behalf."

"How mad are you?"

"How do you quantify anger?"

"I just wanna know how I'm gonna be punished for this." He bared his teeth in a hopeful grimace. "I promise I'll do my penance as long as you're with me."

She shook her head. "I'm not *not* mad. But I'm here, aren't I? Two hours before the show probably isn't a great time to tackle this. But we'll be talking about this a lot in the next few days, I imagine."

"Yeah, there's a lot to talk about." His eyebrows shot up. "Wait, does that mean…"

"I haven't made up my mind yet."

"I didn't think you would," he answered. "Wanna hang out in the bus for a few hours?"

"Like a common groupie." She rolled her eyes, but she looped her arm into his and let him lead her down the hall and out of the venue.

George stood backstage and watched as Macon and his band played their hit album for the femme-heavy audience. She was awed by the easy way he worked the fans. He always seemed to move so effortlessly in everything he did. She'd forgotten how good he was on stage. It was something that, despite all her efforts, just wasn't in her. No amount of will or work allowed her to embody the performer presence that came naturally as walking to Macon. No matter what size stage he was playing, he owned it. He always had. Her heart thumped a little harder, watching him do his job.

She smirked in amusement as a pair of lacy, pink underwear landed on the front of the stage. She leaned out to see the full scope of the crowd. The place was sold out. He finished the set to thunderous screams and applause and stalked off stage behind his bandmates. He made a beeline for George, and she screamed as he dragged her into his arms and pulled her against his sweaty chest.

"Oh my god," she squealed. "You're soaking wet!"

"You love it," he growled, and buried his face in her neck. She clutched his shoulders as he pulled her into a steaming hot kiss that left her weak in the knees. She was so focused on his lips that she didn't realize he was dragging her into the searing brightness and heat of the stage lights. She opened her eyes and gasped against his mouth. He continued pulling her toward center stage even as he finished kissing her. She broke away from his mouth and looked at the crowd with wide eyes. A deafening cheer went up. Macon released her, then sat in the folding chair his roadie had quietly placed in the center of the stage, under a single spotlight, after the last song. He pulled George into his lap, perching her on one of his thighs as he reached around her to adjust the mic and pick up his guitar. George tensed as if to flee, but he held her firmly in place before he trapped her with his guitar.

"Thought I'd do one last song for y'all tonight." The crowd roared. Someone near the stage screamed, *"You, the storm!"*

"*You, the storm?* That what y'all been waiting for?" he asked innocently.

The crowd went wild, and the women in the front rows screamed his name. He jerked his chin at the underwear lying on the stage. "Thank you for the offering." He looked over the nearby fans and shot them a wink and a sexy grin. Whistles and catcalls went up. "But I want to introduce you to *my* storm. This is the voice from my last album that everyone's so crazy about. Including me." He put his lips against her ear. "Whaddya say? Will you sing with me, lover?" He began to pick the opening notes of the song.

George turned her face to look at the biggest crowd she'd ever seen − from this vantage point, at least − and a persistent, deep tremble began in her body. He stopped playing just long enough to reach up and turn her chin gently with his fingers. "Just keep your eyes on me, baby," he murmured as his hands found the strings again.

The hot mic picked up both exchanges, and a ripple of dreamy sighs ran through the audience. George could practically hear the soft sound of panties dropping *en masse*. She had to stifle a giggle, despite being in the grips of the most terrifying and paralyzing stage fright she'd ever experienced. She grounded herself in his eyes until he was all that was left. Nothing and no one else remained to stand between them, not even George herself.

Macon's intense gaze never left her face, even when she closed her eyes and lifted her chin to let her voice free. When their voices wound together and floated through the nearly silent auditorium, something extraordinary happened. Something that felt a lot like magic − the real and rare and tangible kind that has the power to shift the whole world on its axis.

"Babe, do you know where my phone is?"

It had been days since she'd bothered to check it. After all, who would possibly want to call her now that she didn't have the label wanting her time from dawn to dusk? She was surprised at how easy it was for her to abandon it, considering how integral it was to her life up until now. Macon keeping her busy could have had something to do with it. It felt surreal and dreamlike to be on a tour bus with him as they slowly made their way east. He couldn't keep his hands off her, and she didn't want him to. Other than the necessity of getting to his shows, not much was getting done other than Georgia.

She was still pretending to consider the offer he and Lucia presented her. But in her heart, she knew she wouldn't turn it down. It was everything she never knew she wanted until now.

"I put it on the charger in the bunk, Peach."

"Ew, what were you doing with my phone in the bunk?"

"Filling up your camera roll with dick pics," he answered without hesitation.

She laughed. "Oh, perfect."

"No, I found it on the floor earlier. I think it vibrated itself off the table. Judging by how much noise it was making, I thought you might want it charged up before you started catching up on your so-called real life again."

"Huh," she muttered with a bemused expression. "I wonder who's been trying to get in touch. Guess I better check in." She shot him a pointed look as she moved toward the bunk. "And by the way, this is not real life. Being on the road with you isn't any more real than being with you in a cabin that sits in a fairy circle outside of time."

A little smile touched his lips. "Both can be as real as you want."

"Oh no," George said as she looked at her phone with a horrified expression. "Shit, did someone die?" she muttered. Her brow creased as she tried to process the hundreds of text notifications and fifty missed calls. "What. Thee. Fuck," she muttered in alarm.

Macon looked up with a mildly curious expression as she suddenly burst into laughter, then wailed. "Noooo!" She fell back into a seat and put her hands over her face, shaking with laughter.

"What is it? What happened?"

It took her a long minute to pull herself together enough to answer. She read from her screen. "Get you a man who looks at you like Ben Macon looks at his backup singer." She flipped the phone to show him a reel on a social media site. The video had over two-million views. She dropped her phone on the table and put her face in her hands again. "Babe, we've gone viral. Every human being I know is messaging me."

A grin spread across his face. "Lemme see." He slid in next to her and she held up the phone so they could both see the screen. She opened her messages and started playing all the social posts her circle of friends had been sending while she was offline. Their brief stage moment had been captured from hundreds of slightly different angles and was plastered all over every media platform that existed. There was even a version one of the crew must have filmed from backstage, a close-up view of their faces as they sang and gazed into each other's eyes. Seeing herself with him from the outside was intense. They looked so… in love.

"This is mortifying. I have to call Lucia," she said as she stood quickly. She paused and looked down at him as he caught her hand before she could move away. Her eyes softened when she saw the questioning look on his face. "What is it?"

"Don't be mortified. It was beautiful, Georgia. *You're* beautiful."

She blushed and leaned down to press a quick kiss against his mouth. "I'm not ashamed to be seen with you, Makes. I just don't like being seen."

"I know, baby. Maybe we can work on that."

"Maybe."

He tugged her in for one more quick kiss before he released her to reconnect with the world.

George stepped out of the bus and onto the concrete next to the gas pump where they'd stopped for a snack run and fill-up. She was blasted by a wall of cool humidity. The line only rang once before Lucia picked up.

"God, Georgia. Took you long enough to call. Was it planned?" she demanded. "I've been dying over here."

George laughed. "I haven't picked up my phone since before the Denver show."

"Yeah, I fucking bet." Lucia snorted. "The way he carried you off that stage, I was worried his team would have to cancel the rest of the tour dates. Guessing there was no encore that night."

George blushed furiously. "Not for the fans, there wasn't."

Lucia laughed. "Well, watching you two together made

everything pretty clear for me. Even Sharon thought it was hot, and you know how she feels about the muscle boys. We probably watched it fifty times. Absolutely captivating."

George snorted. "That's so embarrassing. And to answer your question – hell no, it wasn't planned. No way I would have agreed if he'd asked ahead of time." On the other side of the call, Lucia made an understanding noise. George shielded her eyes against the bright sun as she paced along the edge of the parking lot. "I won't be doing it again."

"Really?" Lucia sounded slightly disappointed. "You were brilliant, babes. The audience was eating you two up. I thought maybe…"

"Nope," George interrupted in a tone that ended any further discussion. "I'm happy to let Macon do his thing, I don't need to be a part of that."

"On that note, what are you thinking about the proposal?"

George looked back toward the bus. "I haven't told Macon yet, but you probably already knew I was gonna say yes. It's just a lot to work out. Nothing I see in the contract stipulates that Macon has to be involved."

"That's true. You can do this on your own. He knows that. He's prepared for that. This is for you. Your baby."

"Well, I can't imagine not involving him at this point. If he wants."

"Oh, thank fuck. I was biting my nails over here hoping I hadn't made another tactical error." Lucia paused. "I really am sorry, babe."

George sighed. "Everything will be okay, Lucia. With me and Macon, me and you. But I already have some trust issues, so I'm not sure how long it'll take to recover from knowing you two conspired about all this behind my back.

I'm not over it. I really fucking loved that job."

"I know you did, and I loved working with you. You helped build Weber from the ground up. If you think I've forgotten it, you're dead wrong. I don't feel great about how everything went down, George. But we did this because we both care about you. And tell me if I'm wrong, but you're worlds away from where you were before you left. It's only been a couple weeks. Rest. Give it some time to sink in. Any idea where you might want to land?"

"Not yet. That's the biggest thing we have to discuss, between Makes and me." She paused. "If it was up to me, it'd be back in LA, but I know that won't work for him. It's sure as shit not gonna be in Michigan."

"Call me when you figure it out. I'm excited to move forward. Anyway, babes, I have a meeting, so I need to jet. Talk soon?"

"Yeah. Thanks, Lucia. Love you."

"Love you too, babes. I'm glad you're doing better."

George ended the call and walked across the expanse of concrete beyond the gas pumps. Spring was just taking hold. Bloodroot and bluebells bloomed thickly in the ditch that ran along the access road where she stood looking out at the misted green trees and traffic beyond. No, they wouldn't be able to build their studio in the Midwest. It wasn't that there was nothing redeeming about it. George enjoyed plenty of the places she'd passed through and visited in the region. But the thought of staying for more than a few weeks made her want to melt. She felt magnetically repelled by everything east of the Rockies. Any place she couldn't see mountains and have near-constant sunshine just felt wrong.

She hoped she and Macon would be able to find a middle

ground. She hadn't been able to bring herself to initiate the conversation because she was so worried it would fall apart when they actually tried to untangle all the details and turn it into something real. She didn't want to lose him again. But she supposed she didn't have anything or anyone to limit her choices anymore. Macon was waiting patiently and didn't push, but it had to happen sometime.

She looked back at the bus. Maybe today.

Immerensis

(n.) The maddening inability to understand the reasons
why someone loves you—almost as if you're selling them
a used car that you know has a ton of problems and
requires daily tinkering just to get it to run normally, but
no matter how much you try to warn them, they seem all
the more eager to hop behind the wheel and see where
this puppy can go.

The realtor smiled and gave a little wave as she got back into her car and steered it away, down the long drive. The road would lead her past the big gray pines that bracketed the route at this altitude, around the big barn. At this height, it was in the low 80s under the pines, despite the summer heat that shimmered on the desert floor spreading out from the base of the mountain property. Almost a thousand feet lower, pines would give way to scrub oak, then to a grove of pecans as the land started to flatten out. The final stretch of the long road wound under the arching, green branches of the Palo Verde trees until it reached the two-lane road that led back to the highway. Beyond, the late afternoon sun lit the bare mountains in the distance with soft pastels. George took a deep breath of the clean, desert air.

She turned to Macon. "What do you think?"

He looked around thoughtfully. "I never really 'got' the

desert." He took a deep breath. "But I see the appeal. It's quiet. It smells nice. It's like the wind has scoured away all the memories and distractions. The view is incredible. And I like these mountainous parts where there are some big trees. I need big trees."

"I agree," George agreed. "I… know this sounds weird, but I feel like it's already ours. Like I'm supposed to be here. We're only a half day's drive from LA. We're still in California. Ticks a lot of boxes for me. We'd have a pecan grove, and we'd be on our own aquifer."

He took her hand and gave it a little tug. "Let's go look at the barn again. Give some thought as to how we might fill out the space. Also, that little adobe house off the pecans – we could live there full time. We could build musician housing up here near the studio and still be far enough away that we'd have a lot of privacy. Pretty cool to have a whole mountain right in the backyard, too."

"I just worry a little bit about up-keep. Eighty acres seems like a lot."

"We can handle it." He leaned down to kiss her temple. "If you want this place, that is."

"Will it be inconvenient for you to be this far out when you need to leave for the next tour?"

He looked down at her with a puzzled expression. "We talked about this, love. I'm done. This was it for me."

"I guess I just thought… like. Your career is peaking right now."

"Yeah," he agreed. "Which makes it the perfect time to bow out."

"That's not really how it works. You're supposed to seize this moment and capitalize on it. This project doesn't need to stand in your way. I can manage while you're gone."

He looked out at the mountains. "Nah. I'm not chasing that shit. Besides, it'd drive me shit crazy to leave you behind for half of every year."

"You're making all the sacrifices, here. I don't wanna keep you here. Or keep you from something that you're really fucking good at, Macon. Something that you love."

"Baby, I *want* this. I was already considering this even before you came back into my life," he said softly. "Besides, it's not like we won't be making music. *That's* what I love." He squeezed her and looked down his nose at her face. "And you. That's what matters."

———

Macon found Georgia cleaning up a trash-filled shed down the hill from the barn. Summer was waning, and here under the pines, they hovered on the brink of hoodie weather. Down the hill, it was still warm enough to take advantage of the temporary outdoor shower he made for them behind their little house. As soon as they closed on the property, Macon got crews in and started the work renovating the barn, and all of them had been going full bore all summer to beat the fall rains.

He dragged her away to show her the nearly finished studio, from which she'd been banished for the past several days. The wood floors were in. The newly installed wall panels gleamed with a fresh coat of finish. George ran her fingers over the smooth surfaces.

"Oh, it's so pretty," she breathed. "I love this gray wood."

"I had the crew upcycle it from that old barn that was falling down on the neighbor's property. They gave us all the wood in exchange for taking the mess off their land. Got some other stuff we can use. Old farm sink. Some cool, old signs."

"I adore it. Good job, babe."

"I think we'll be operational within two months." Macon pulled her into his body. "You excited?"

"Wildly." She lifted her chin and kissed his neck. "Honestly, I'm more excited we'll finally be able to start working on our house." An electric thrill rippled through her at the thought. She dreamed this wish, once. It didn't look like the cabin in Michigan. It wasn't LA. It looked like something new for both of them, something they could build together, that would just be theirs.

"Me too." He stole another kiss, then set her free.

"Since you've let me back in, I'm gonna paint the bathroom, and then I can be done for the day." She stood on her tiptoes to kiss his jaw, and he slipped his hands into the sides of her loose overalls to pull her hips into his body again. She laughed and pushed him away.

"I'm gonna clean up the sound booths while you work." He pushed her toward the bathroom and smacked her ass as she walked away. She looked back at him and shook her head in mock disapproval.

Almost an hour later, she dropped the roller into the paint tray and yawned. She felt a presence at her back and turned straight into Macon's chest. She looked up and found him hovering over her with a hungry look in his eyes. "What? Why are you looking at me like that?"

"I'm ready to get you home." He snagged one strap of her overalls and pulled her close. "I've been wanting to take these off you all day."

George grinned. "Why wait?"

"Crew's still here."

"They're almost done loading up. I don't think they're coming back. Besides, that's why we installed soundproof booths, right? Isn't that why we put those in?"

"Good point. That is exactly why we have them." He reached up and deftly snapped the clasps of her overall straps open and manhandled her across the room as she laughed and yanked at the buttons on the front of his shirt. He pulled her into one of the new sound booths and closed the door behind them.

No one came up looking for them, but had they, they wouldn't have heard a sound. However, they might have seen the steamy outline of George's palm pressed flat against the small glass window in the sound booth door, and Macon's much larger one covering it.

Solla, Solla, Solla

(n.) An incantation whispered privately to yourself to celebrate the loss of something or someone you loved, consciously deciding to relinquish them to an earlier part of your life.

The mountains were dusted with snow and George's breath was thick in the air on the early November morning when she pulled down the long drive to the farm roads, then access roads, then to the 14 Freeway as she headed back to LA. She thought when they bought the place and started building the recording studio, she'd want to be back in LA as much as possible. But after just a month living there full-time, going back rarely occurred to her. She spent most of her days working alongside Macon and the construction crew. Evenings were spent resting, reclining against Macon's chest in the hammock, watching the sun set over the mountains and the vast expanse of high desert around them. When the season changed, they wrapped their limbs up together and read books by the wood burning stove or picked the strings of one of their many instruments.

This morning, it was a struggle to tear herself from Macon's possessive embrace in their big, warm bed and stumble into the predawn cold to shower. She wasn't excited to be going back to LA, but she was happy she'd see Lucia and all the other faces she missed. She wasn't sure why she had to meet with Weber on this particular day, but they were bankrolling the studio build, so she figured she should make a trip in. She planned on hitting a couple of her favorite ethnic markets to restock on much-missed spices and ingredients that weren't available in their rural region before she headed back. Macon encouraged her to stay overnight, but she already knew she'd rather have a sixteen-hour day than spend a night without him.

She thought they would have cooled off a little, but after eight months, he still looked at her the way he did that first night, after he brought her in from the storm and warmed up her frozen heart.

She supposed they had a lot of lost time to make up for. And after so much loss, this thing between them, the intensity of their love for each other, was precious. She didn't have any desire to turn it down or let it cool.

She thought how her luck just never seemed to run out. Lucky Georgia. Having this life with this man was the luckiest and most unexpected gift yet.

It was still gorgeous and a crisp fifty degrees in LA, and George reveled in the bright, warm sunshine after a week of rain and chill in the desert mountains. Magenta bougainvillea still bloomed in thick mats all over town, and the ever-green palms and tropical trees seemed so absurdly verdant and cheery after months in pastel mountains punctuated only by dark pines and somber junipers.

She pulled into the parking garage and shivered at the feeling that rolled over her. It was so remarkably familiar that she almost felt as though she'd driven right back into her old life.

She tensed at the thought. No part of her wanted it back. It was shocking how rapidly her life and goals transformed after she met Macon. It was gratitude for all those changes in her life, and not a sense of what she'd lost, that she felt as she entered the elevator and ascended to the top floor of Weber Records.

The vibes were expectant and tense when George arrived in her old office space. Misha and Blake greeted her excitedly. Two other women were sitting with Lucia in a closed-door meeting. Her eyes briefly flicked to George through the glass wall of her office, and she lifted her fingers in a small wave before continuing to talk.

"What's going on?" George asked Blake.

"We're waiting for the call," Misha said and bared her teeth in an excited smile. "It's so good to see you, George! How's life at the studio?"

"It's good – what call are you talking about?"

"I'll wait for Lucia to tell you. What route did you take into town?"

"The 405 to Sunset, why?"

"Damn, you missed it all, then." Misha pouted.

George rolled her eyes and put her hands on her hips. "Misha. Just tell me what's going on. What did I miss? Who are the people in Lucia's office, what call are we waiting on? I order you. As… as an *elder*."

Blake laughed and Misha bounced with barely contained glee. "Okay, I can tell you part of it. That's Macon's publicity team with Lucia. And if you'd come across town from the other side, you probably would have seen more than one billboard featuring your hot-ass boyfriend on your way in."

George's eyebrows shot up. "Are you telling me…?"

"Listen," Misha interrupted. "It's not my fault if you manage to extrapolate something more from what I just told you. But I can't tell you anything else." She made a motion like she was zipping her mouth closed.

"They've been campaigning for a Grammy."

Misha just shrugged. "Couldn't say. Wanna see the creative for the billboards?"

George dropped her bag on Blake's desk and stood behind Misha as she pulled up the files.

"Oh my god." On the left began a dark spiral of pine branches laid flat, overlaid with white text. Same as the album cover. But the image extended to the right, into a dark, moody, black and white of Macon. He was curled into a bed of pine branches, shirtless, with tattered jeans low on his hips, his sculpted torso slightly opened to the viewer, his bottom arm extended to the left as if he was reaching for something.

Misha grinned at her intake of breath and the way she drank in the image with wide eyes. "I know, right? I told you it was hot. I wonder if these have caused any accidents yet."

"Seriously," George murmured. "Where's the closest one? I wanna get a picture before I head home."

"I'll send you a pin."

George looked up as multiple voices spilled into the room from Lucia's office. The two publicists and Lucia strolled out into the space. The two women took up the rest of the available chairs and Lucia pulled George into a hug before she sat next to her on the edge of Misha's desk.

"Blake!" she shouted, and Blake popped up. "Coffee

orders, please." He saluted and approached the others, and Misha went to help him. Lucia looked George over with a grin. "Goddamn, you look great. I swear you lost ten years."

"I feel it," George admitted. "I don't think I realized how overtaxed my nervous system was in the city. Quiet suits me."

Lucia cocked an eyebrow. "So does the lumberjack. Spend much time on social media these days?"

"Just the studio accounts. I've been doing teasers for the opening. But I don't scroll much anymore, why?"

"You two are still circulating. People are still eating up the love story." Lucia nudged George with her elbow.

"That's sweet, I guess. Weird, but sweet." George shot Lucia a puzzled expression.

"He's gonna get a nomination, George. I feel it in my bones."

"God, thank you so much. I was getting annoyed, not being able to talk about it. I was sworn to secrecy." George heaved a relieved sigh.

Lucia rolled her eyes. "Misha's a fucking idiot. I told her not to tell you just because I knew she would if I got stuck in that meeting. At least she's a predictable tool."

George laughed. "So, what's the deal? I had no idea this was happening."

"Macon knew."

George's smile fell away. "Really?"

"Well, he gave the approval back in June. He didn't really want to know any of the particulars. Figured it couldn't hurt the studio's esteem to try for a nomination."

"Huh. Well, that makes sense. Sounds like Makes."

"Did Misha show you the billboard art?"

"Yeah, damn." George took a bracing breath as her cheeks flushed with heat. "I've never seen the photos from that shoot."

"We did them the day you two reconnected. You should have seen the fight he put up when we wanted to shave that beard off."

George grinned. "The beard is back, but I've got it in check."

"You two are good, I take it? You look amazing."

"More than good."

Lucia eyed her shrewdly. "This life you've clawed out for yourself is pretty sweet."

"I've always been lucky, I guess." George shrugged.

"Oh, Georgia." Lucia smiled softly. "Luck had nothing to do with this. You built this brick by brick."

George felt her eyes well up, and she turned away to touch the corners of them with her sleeve. Blake and Misha arrived back, and the moment broke and turned into something more festive as they delivered coffee to their grateful colleagues.

"Blake," George crooned. "You remembered I like a mint mocha when it's cold." She pouted sweetly. "That's so sweet, buddy."

"'Course I did, George." Blake smiled. "You're unforgettable."

The publicist's phone jangled loudly, and George was saved from having to respond. She and Lucia both jumped.

George turned to Lucia and made big eyes as if to say, "Who uses a ringer like that?" Lucia's mouth quirked in amusement, but both of them held their breath as the woman took the call.

"Brenda Lee," the woman answered crisply, and the space fell silent. Misha sat on the edge of her seat, trying to listen in on the conversation, but Brenda was giving them nothing on her end, and her earbuds were sound tight.

After several *mmhmms* and a few *okays* and *alrights*, Brenda ended the call. She looked up with a flat face. "He got four nominations." She broke into a wide smile as George, Lucia, Misha, and Blake all jumped up and screamed simultaneously, like their favorite team just scored a goal.

"FOUR!" Lucia crowed. Across the room, Misha pulled Blake into a surprise kiss, to which she found him quite receptive.

George made her way to the long couch at the opposite side of the office and fell into it. Her face wore a dazed expression. After a few minutes, Lucia joined her.

"Stay in town tonight. Sharon wants to see you. You can sleep in our spare room."

"Oh, no. I have to go back right away. I have to tell Macon. I'm not even gonna stop at the Armenian market. I had a whole day planned."

"Macon made me promise I'd figure out how to keep you here until tomorrow."

George's jaw dropped. "Jesus fuck, Lucia! How often do you two talk?"

Lucia grinned. "He emails me when he needs to communicate." She sighed. "Please don't fight me on this George. I promised him." She gave George a pointed look. "I'm sure he's trying to do something nice and you're gonna ruin the surprise if you don't back the fuck off."

George groaned. "Fine. I can't believe I have to sit with this for twenty-four hours."

"Don't be a codependent bitch. We're taking you out to dinner with our friends. And we miss you. It'll be nice to spend some time, just us girls."

George spent a brilliant night laughing with Sharon, Lucia, and a gaggle of their women friends, all in the forty-to-six-ty range, power players in various niches of the LA entertainment industries. She remembered how much she loved being amid groups of women like this. The last time she alighted in this particular way was when she was hanging out with Aunt Carla's coven in the week before the funeral. She made a commitment to them to come back quarterly for their meetup. Even still, she was all too ready to leave by the time she woke up on Wednesday.

A little pulse of excitement beat through her as she climbed out of bed, like waking up on Christmas, or the last day of school. It wasn't that she *couldn't* be without him. She just didn't *want* to. She dressed and hurried into the living room. She groaned when she turned the corner and spotted Sharon and Lucia sitting at their kitchen table, smiling at her expectantly. Sharon peered over her readers and set the paper she was perusing on the table. She patted the chair next to her.

"Come on, dear. Have a cup of coffee with us. I made homemade rhubarb-cheesecake strudel," she cajoled.

George sighed and sat down. "I can't say no to your strudel, Sharon." She looked at Lucia. "Is this part of it? Can I just ask when I'm allowed to go home so I can plan accordingly?"

Lucia grinned. "He said not to let you leave before noon."

"Oh, my god," George muttered. "I need to go shopping

before I leave town, so I'm still gonna head out soon." Sharon placed a cup of coffee and a plate full of strudel in front of George. George's face melted with delight as she tasted it. "Okay, this was super worth staying for."

"What are we doing in the way of shopping today?" Lucia asked. "Anything I'd want to come along for? It'd be nice to get some more time with you."

George grinned. "If you want. I'm headed to Burbank. I have to make a stop at Ikea because I need to get like, half a pallet of pillar candles. There's a boutique closer to NoHo that sells handmade lingerie, and while I'm over there, there's a chocolatier I wanna hit."

Lucia's eyebrows shot up. "Alright, that's hot."

Sharon looked up from her paper with interest. "I'm coming too."

"You two are shameless, you know that?" George shook her head and got to work finishing her strudel.

Limerance

(n.) The overwhelming emotional experience of being
in love, in which the object of affection occupies nearly
every thought and dominates one's feelings.

The old, green truck emerged from the pecan grove along the edge of the scrub oaks. It bumped along the small dirt road that cut through the property and rumbled to a stop next to George's silver Subaru, which was already parked in front of the small, adobe house. A huge, gnarled, old pine tree arched large branches over the home and little dirt yard.

The sun was already behind the mountain and evening was slipping over the desert, pushing a chilly breeze ahead of it.

Macon disembarked from the truck with a little smile and jogged to the front door. He pushed it open to find the interior dark, but glowing with candlelight and filled with low music. His eyes ran around the room until they landed on George. His eyebrows shot up. She waited for him on the couch, knees spread, wearing only her red glasses, red heels, and a strappy, complicated network of ribbons, straps, and thin strips of lace in red. Despite how much of her body it covered, it managed to cover virtually nothing.

He exhaled heavily. "Holy hell, Peaches," he murmured.

"Have you come to take my soul?"

She beckoned to him with two fingers. "Get over here immediately, Bennett Macon the Third."

He obeyed quickly and knelt between her knees. "Either I got it and you're rewarding me, or I didn't and you're consoling me." He took her thighs in his hands and kneaded them lightly with his thumbs. "Either way, I do not give one hot fuck. I'm gonna take you to bed and tie you up with all those ribbons." He scooped her up before she could protest and carried her to their room, where candles were also already lit. A bottle of Martinelli's apple cider protruded from the ice in a bucket near the headboard. A platter of chocolate covered strawberries sat in the middle of their low palette bed.

"I hope you don't expect me to stop and eat," he growled.

"I'll feed you those later if you're very, very good," she whispered into his ear, and he groaned.

"I'm about to take you apart with my fuckin' teeth, Georgia." He wanted to toss her on the bed but summoned all his will to restrain himself long enough to save the strawberries. After he moved them to the dresser, he dove into the bed with her and pulled her back into the fluffy comforter. She giggled as he grabbed her up, his teeth moving along her neck.

She squirmed in his grasp until she was nose-to-nose with him. "Babe." She brought her hands to his cheeks and cupped them with cool fingers. "You were nominated in four categories."

He froze. "That's… unexpected." His face cycled through a variety of emotions.

George pressed a soft kiss on his lips. "Congratulations."

It took several seconds for him to recover from the news. He blinked and the glazed look left his eyes. "Anyway," he said with a shrug. She squealed as he dove face-first into her breasts and ran his tongue over one of her nipples through a bit of lace.

George sighed and watched as he worked his way down her body, pulling all the catchments of her lingerie free as his mouth traveled over her skin. She was panting by the time he had her opened up like a gift. He left her just long enough to yank off his shirt and pants before burning hot kisses along her ribs and over her flat belly. When he hit her bellybutton, his tongue began its slow descent until he was lapping softly at her pearl.

She moaned as she tugged his hair. "Come up here. I don't want to wait." She felt him smile against her briefly before he moved slowly back up her body, taking his time with his mouth to her impatient groans of protest.

He paused to press his forehead against her belly. He took a deep breath of her scent and sighed. "I missed you, Peaches."

George's body pulsed with fire and need by the time his lips found hers. He brought her arms over her head and pinned them there, then pressed the length of his body against hers. He slowly pulled one of the long ribbons of her negligee through all the loops and eyelets keeping it in place. It slid along her skin, scratching gently along her ribs, her back, and slipping over her nipples as he pulled it free. He looped it around her wrists, still caught in the grip of his other hand, and made quick work of tying them together firmly. She tugged gently at the ribbon and her eyes widened when she realized he'd connected the binding to the headboard.

He watched her with a sexy, little smirk for a few seconds and rumbled his approval as she realized her hands weren't going anywhere.

She groaned and arched against his body. "Macon!" she protested.

"Now I can work without interference."

Her answering giggle turned into a strangled moan as he picked up where he left off. Soon, he had her gasping and arching and digging her heels into the soft bed. It was only after she begged that he released her wrists and let George do exactly what she wanted.

He held her hips as she slowly rose and fell over him, her eyes locked on his, the loose satin ribbons tickling him where they slid over his chest. When she finally succumbed to the thick, hot pressure where they connected, her head fell back and a low moan ripped from her throat. Macon's breath caught in his chest as he watched her face. He didn't believe in gods, but there was something holy, something that felt sacred about their bodies together. Like they'd kindled some ancient magic out of sleep. He waited until she leaned limply against his chest before he arched into her with a groan and gritted teeth as he took his own, intense release. He spread soft kisses all over her face.

"Do you know how good you are?" he whispered against her cheek.

Mmm, Georgia hummed. "I'm glad you know."

"So, all this is just because of the Grammy thing?"

She laughed and pushed herself off his chest with weak arms. She looked down at him with a fond expression. "The Grammy thing." She cocked an eyebrow at him. "It has nothing to do with that. I just wanted to make sure you weren't missing your time on the road. Make sure you're happy here at home."

He laughed, and his eyes crinkled up in a way that made George's heart flutter. "Shit like this definitely wasn't happening on the road, baby." His face got serious. "Not at all. Not with me."

She smiled softly. "I'm not judging you, Macon. I didn't have any ownership of you. I know what happens on tours."

His eyebrows shot up. "I'm serious. I was celibate for about five years when you came along." On her shocked face, he added, "Not by any kind of commitment or plan."

"Why, then?" She pushed a sweaty lock of hair off his forehead and ran a soft finger down his cheek.

"After Mel, I went a little wild. 'Seeking life-affirming experiences,' as my shrink said. For a while it helped drown out the worst of the loneliness. A couple years of that and I realized how much lonelier it made me at the end of the day. Over time, the pain of the aftermath conditioned me not to want any part of it. And when I tried, I couldn't… ahhh… perform."

She frowned. "That's… fairly impossible to imagine."

He laughed softly. "So anyway, I just stopped trying. It became *a thing*. It felt healthy. I channeled more of my vital energy into my music."

"But what about…" She blushed softly.

He grinned. "What were you gonna say?"

"Never mind."

He squeezed her hip. "Come on."

"Why did you have condoms at the cabin if you were celibate?"

He burst out laughing and his whole body shook as she

smirked down at him. "An abundance of optimism?" he offered after he caught his breath. "Goddamn, Peaches. You are such a jealous…" He pulled her down into his body and nipped at her ear. "Little…" he said close to her neck, and she shivered. "Brat," he finished, then planted a quick, hot kiss on her lips to muffle her protest. "I picked them up when I went into town to send Lucia the files on the library WiFi."

"No, you didn't!"

"I did."

"Because of *me*," she stated flatly. "Because you were *that* confident I was going to sleep with you, you decided to break five years of celibacy."

He burst out laughing again. "What do you want me to say, Georgia? You *did* sleep with me." He took a moment to finish laughing and squeezed her hips. "Do you know how many times I had to go chop wood to get away from you, or go to bed with a raging hard-on because you were on the other side of my bedroom door? I wasn't about to get caught out if you initiated something."

She blushed.

"You were jealous of phantoms, baby." He tilted his head and gazed at her with a little smile. "That first morning, when I realized who you were…" His eyes ran over her face as he remembered. "There was bright light coming in through the front window of the cabin, and when you turned around, it was at the back of your head. And your bun was falling down." He reached up and threaded his fingers into the hair at her neck. "The sun was catching in your bedhead and lighting up all the loose little strands. Like you were wearing a platinum halo. Standing there in my shirt, you looked like a fuckin' angel. I just thought, 'Uh oh.

Look at this beautiful bit of trouble who just landed in my nest.'"

She ducked her chin shyly and he tilted it back up with gentle fingers.

"That was the first time I felt anything at all in such a long time, Georgia. Except maybe when I was making music. You hit me like a lightning bolt. You made my bones hurt. You confused my heart. I kept thinking it was such a bad idea to even be friendly with you after what happened with me and Mel. You broke me down the second you said you believed me out on the lake."

Georgia blinked. "I… I had no idea."

"I felt terrible when you told me what happened with Kato that day at your aunt's funeral. My heart hurt for you, so badly. For about two hours of my drive back." He smirked. "Then I turned on the stereo, and you know what came on the college radio station?" He paused to chuckle. "On some throwback night, no less…"

She laughed. "Oh no, what was it?"

"Such Great Heights."

"That was just like… 2004-ish. How is that a throwback?"

He grinned. "Twenty-one years ago, baby."

She made a disgusted noise.

"Anyway, that came on…"

"Which version?"

"Postal Service," he said with a laugh. "Are you gonna let me finish my story? I'm telling you how I fell in love with you, Georgia Lane."

She laughed lightly and smiled down at him with soft eyes. "Go on."

"SO. That came on." He pursed his lips and waited for

her to interrupt. She giggled. "And I thought about how sweet it would be to know you were waiting for me at the end of a tour. By the time I got home, the idea of leaving our entirely imaginary relationship to go on tour seemed incomprehensible. It took me three hours to write *You, The Storm*. I stayed up all night recording. We hadn't even gotten together, and you'd already broken my heart."

George opened and closed her mouth several times. "Macon," she whispered, "that's the most romantic thing anyone's ever said to me."

"When you stormed off that day, I was so fucking angry with myself. I was so mad and hurt, and then… there you were. I had a second chance, and I wasn't going to be a coward about it."

"Lucky me," whispered Georgia. She was still slightly stunned by his words. "I'm not mad anymore… but, since we're on the subject. If you felt that way, why didn't you try to get in touch?"

The corners of his mouth turned up in a sad, little, rueful smile. "I'd like to show you something. An exhibit in my defense, if you will."

"Okay…?"

He lifted her off his chest and swung her over into the other side of the bed. "I need to get my laptop, be right back."

He padded out of the room naked, and Georgia watched him go with an appreciative sigh. He crawled back into bed with her and she sat up. He pulled up his email and scrolled around looking for something.

"Here it is." He put the computer in her lap. "My only defense."

Georgia read the email open on the screen. It was from lucia@weberrecords.la.

Macon, Leave Georgia alone. Let her heal from this shit storm of recent tragedy in her life. It's not fair for you to sweep her off her feet with your hard abs, croony little ballads, and that whole moody, tortured artist shit you have going on. She doesn't have a lot left to anchor her right now, other than her job. I swear on the goddess, herself, that I will castrate you if you help her trash her career at this vulnerable time.

Darling, the album is gorgeous, by the way. We're really looking forward to releasing these tracks.

-L

George's mouth was hanging open when she finished. "Damn, babe. That's lowkey terrifying. But I still don't undertsand why you listened to her."

He nodded and stashed the laptop on the side of the bed. "I know. But every time I thought about you, I thought about that email. And I don't think she was wrong, in theory, that's the thing. It was kind of a creep move to get involved with someone who was dealing with such a spectacular mess. She was right. Good sense said to let you be. But good sense doesn't have much to do with love. I should have known better."

George slid down onto her back and stared at the flickering candlelight on the ceiling. "Don't you ever leave me behind again."

"I'm gonna wife you and you won't be able to get rid

of me, ever." He turned on his side and propped himself up on his elbow.

"Is that so? Don't tell me you already got a ring, because you're so confident I'll want to marry you," she teased.

"Yeah, it's around here somewhere," he said with a little smile. "I wanna be able to say, 'unhand my wife,' or 'that's my WIFE.' Things like that."

She laughed, and Macon rolled away from her to reach for his pants, crumpled on the floor near the bed. He rifled around in the pockets before emerging with a little, black, velvet box. He handed it to her, and she shot him a quizzical expression as she sat up to open it.

She stared at the dime-sized stone of the diamond solitaire ring nestled into the black velvet within for a full minute before she rediscovered her ability to speak.

"You were serious."

"Of course I was serious, Georgia."

She looked up at him, her brown-gold eyes catching the firelight like polished tigers-eye. "You know there's no one else in the world I wanna be with." She looked down at the ring again. "I just don't know if I want marriage anymore. My last attempt at being engaged ended rather dramatically."

He took a deep breath. "I won't be able to say all the wife stuff."

"Is this why I wasn't allowed to come home until today?"

"Yeah," he sighed. "I got stuck in a road closure coming back from the jeweler. I had a bag full of candles and a shit ton of flowers in the truck, but you beat me home."

She reached up to cup his cheek. "Oh, babe. I'm sorry I ruined your surprise."

"You don't have anything to apologize for, my love."

"You know you're imprinted on my DNA, right? I'm not going anywhere."

"I know, baby." He leaned in and kissed her softly. "Can we eat the strawberries now? I'm starving."

Georgia burst out in surprised laughter and clambered out of bed to fetch the tray of chocolate-covered berries. "You're not upset?" she asked as she crawled back into bed carefully with the tray.

"Nope. Because next time I ask, I'll have spoiled you so thoroughly you won't be able to say no."

"To be clear," she said as she held a berry to his lips, "I didn't actually say no. I just need some time to think."

"There's hope yet," he said through a mouthful of fruit and chocolate.

"Shhh," she soothed, and pushed another strawberry into his mouth until it was too full for him to speak.

Eudaemonia

(n.) Realizing one's full potential and engaging in mean-
ingful activities, representing the highest human good and
a lasting sense of thriving.

January blew in with brutally cutting winds that swept across the desert floor, rushed through the tall pines by the studio, and howled over the boulders. The little adobe house was situated in a fortuitous position between the two extremes and in the protective embrace of two opposite, rocky ridges between the evergreen scrub oaks and bare pecan orchard.

George was stirring a large cast iron pot of posole when Macon entered on a blast of frigid air. He threw his coat on the hook and moved quickly to her side to warm himself. "It's 18 degrees out there. It's supposed to snow tonight. I hope we don't have any trouble getting out tomorrow."

"It'll melt by midday. It always does." She finished stirring and balanced the wood spoon across the rim of the pot. "We don't have to be in LA until Wednesday, technically, so we can leave as late as we need to tomorrow."

He wrapped his arms around her. "I was just in a virtual meeting with the team before I wrapped up at the studio."

"Yeah? What's going on?"

"Well, they had this really interesting idea about the

performance and wanted me to run it by you." He brought one of his hands up and ran it over her hair. His other hand tightened at the small of her back, and he pulled her in for a slow, sweet kiss.

She pulled away and leaned back, her eyes narrowing. "Mixing business with pleasure? Sir, why are you trying to butter me up? What did Lucia say to you?" Her alarm increased when he didn't laugh. "Macon!"

"Hear me out, okay?"

She tried to unwrap his arms from her waist and he squeezed her more tightly. "There's only one thing you could be asking me that would warrant this kind of behavior, and it's so unhinged that I know it can't possibly be what I'm thinking."

"They want you to sing with me. *I* want you to sing with me."

"That is the exact thing I thought was so unhinged that you wouldn't even think to repeat it to me." She wiggled out of his arms and put her hands on her hips.

"Georgia. Please let me say my piece."

"With the understanding that I won't be swayed. But go ahead, I'll listen." She gestured for him to continue.

"Come here." He caught her hand and led her to the couch. He pulled her down into his lap.

"You're not gonna change my mind just by cuddling me like a big, sexy bear," she stated firmly. Macon wrapped his arms around her midsection and clasped his hands over her belly. She rested her hands on his and glanced down as the firelight caught on a facet of the obscenely large stone on her left ring finger. She snuggled back against his chest and let her eyes wander over the room. It was warm with firelight and candlelight. In the darkest days of December, Macon replastered the old walls and put in new wood flooring from extra reclaimed barn wood. Thick rugs on the floor and the warm glow bouncing from the row of wall-mounted guitars gave the room a homey and welcoming feel. Across the open space, Macon had installed a long, heavy, butch-er-block oak slab countertop and matching farmhouse table that he milled himself from reclaimed burn-area timber. The vintage farmhouse sink was set into the counter. It was a beautiful home he'd made for them here. Her life with Macon was idyllic, largely because of his tireless efforts. She could suffer to hear him.

She sighed. "Go ahead. Make your case."

"We're doing a mashup of five songs. Each performance will segue into the next continuously. They want us in the number three spot, right in the middle of it all." He paused and rubbed his hands slowly up and down her arms.

She tilted her chin up and twisted to look up at him. "I'm sorry, were you expecting me to respond? That's a lineup, not a case for why I should participate."

"I explained the issue and the production designer had an idea. You can meet him on Wednesday at rehearsal. I want him to tell you what we could do. You'll be there anyway, it couldn't hurt."

"Can I get the Cliff's Notes, at least?"

"He thought of a way that you won't have to see the audience. You'll only see me. And we'll be backed by a small choir, and an orchestra section. I won't even be playing. I'll just be standing in a little bubble with you."

Her brows drew together. "Okay, well… just for the sake of understanding what the fuck that even means, I will hear your designer." She twisted around and rearranged her legs until she was sitting upright across his lap. "Are you doing the arrangement for the orchestra?"

He smiled softly and ran the back of his finger down her jawline. "You know, you're a lot more grounded since we moved here, Peach."

She cocked an eyebrow at him. "You've only known me at the most ungrounded times in my life. You missed the whole middle part where I was owning and winning."

"That's fair. But I don't think you'd be asking about orchestral arrangements if you were about to fall apart because I've suggested this."

"You're right. I'm in the best place I've ever been. You're largely to blame for that. You *do* understand I'm not agreeing to anything, right? I'm just curious. I'm not singing in front of live studio audience of thirteen-thousand people."

"Okay, baby."

"You think because of this…" She held her hand out and made her ring sparkle in the low light. It was the sole ring on both her hands now. "You think I'll always come around to your way if you let me think long enough. I just don't want you to be disappointed when I say no."

"I won't."

The four-day trip to LA was a whirlwind of rehearsals, dinners, and lots of new faces. George found it enjoyable, but exhausting after the pace of their much slower desert life. On the first day, the production designer, Matieu, sat with her in the venue's theater seating and explained his concept as the musical acts and stand-ins for the hosts rehearsed below them.

"Also, the white LED pattern we'll project up the silk will look like glowing rain. That'll help obscure your view of everything around you, too. And it'll be *sooo* pretty. As long as you keep eye contact with him the whole time, you won't see a thing. It'll feel like you're inside a solid column of moving light. I don't have a full prototype built, but I've done enough testing with the materials to know it'll work."

"What about getting to the platform? I'll have to walk straight toward the audience."

"He should carry you. Referential to the original moment. Close your eyes until he gets to your marks, open them when he puts you down and you're facing him."

George said she needed time to think, but Matieu wanted an answer within twenty-four hours to make sure he had time to incorporate the build, and so George could run through the rehearsals while they were in town.

He patted her arm kindly, then left her sitting in the middle of the auditorium as he returned to work. She chewed her lip thoughtfully as she stared at his number in her phone. It was Macon's moment. She wanted to give him something. She just wished it was anything but this. She wished she had more time to think about it.

She looked down at her engagement ring and considered she'd do just about anything that would make him happy. Within reason. She wasn't sure if this was within reason.

She thought about the way he fed her when she was dying for him, and how he constantly showed his love for her in a hundred little actions. She wanted to support him, and she knew how much he wanted her to say yes, even though he wasn't pushing her.

What if she physically couldn't sing? It would be *wild* to

ruin the Grammys. To derail the big ensemble performance of the night with crippling stage fright. That would not be the cherry atop Macon's big performance. She just didn't want to fuck everything up for everyone.

She sighed and looked at her phone. She opened her messaging app and tapped out a quick note. She stared at it for several long seconds, then sent it. She leaned back in her seat and let her breath out in relief. At least she wouldn't have to sit there, burdened with the terror of an impossible decision any longer.

She was pensive at dinner with Sharon and Lucia that night. Macon chattered with them effortlessly as they ate. He glanced over to see her pushing her food around on her plate and reached under the table to squeeze her knee. She looked up at him and he smiled softly, leaving his hand on her leg as he continued the conversation. She was busy making a little dome of arugula over her grilled potatoes, deep in thought, when Macon double-squeezed her thigh.

"Depends on what George wants," he was saying.

She looked up sheepishly. "I was zoning out. What were you asking?"

Lucia pinned her with a piercing look. "What are you doing for the wedding?"

"Oh! I hadn't thought much about it." She pursed her lips. "Maybe just a little courthouse thing. I don't want to make a fuss."

Macon and Lucia shared a silent look of commiseration.

"She's always like this," he said.

"Don't I know it," said Lucia. She turned to George. "Under no circumstance… Georgia! Stop playing with your food and look at me. Under no circumstance are you not having a wedding."

"I don't need to have a grown-up prom," she argued. "I'm just doing this because Macon really wants to call me 'wife.'" Next to her, he shook his head and smirked.

Sharon rolled her eyes. "You'll have a small wedding at the studio. We'll get Joe Bones's crew down there to produce the event. You don't have to do anything. Seventy-five people, max."

Macon cut in. "If we build a couple cottages around the studio where we were talking about making the band quarters, we could rent out the space for weddings. It'd probably make as much in a weekend as we bill the bands for a week of engineering."

"We're on the same page, Muscles," answered Sharon. "This will be a good test run. We'll have to find some local suppliers for the setup." Sharon pulled a notebook out of her bag and started taking notes. "I'll start putting together a list of people we need to call."

"Thirty people, max," Georgia said, and they all stopped and looked at her as if they'd forgotten she was there.

Lucia patted her hand. "We can talk numbers later, dear."

George put her face in her hands as her three companions continued to plot her wedding independently of her. Macon stroked her leg softly under the table and threw her reassuring smiles every now and again, and Georgia finally relaxed and ate her dinner.

Let them plot, she thought. It felt nice to leave planning to the more interested parties. She had quite enough on her mind already.

28

Dorgone

(adj.) Wondering if you could slip away from an event
or group conversation without anyone noticing your
absence.

George's heart was beating furiously. They waited back-stage as the first set of performers took their places on stage and the lights went up. She couldn't fathom what had possessed her to agree to this. It was absolute madness. She still had time to run. She could duck into a bar on the boulevard and they'd never find her. The doors leading out into the loading area were tantalizingly close.

She looked over at Macon. He was dressed in a bougie version of what he was wearing when they had their viral moment in Denver. His worn jeans were tight, designer, artfully torn and worn. The t-shirt was tight, white, and tailored perfectly to show off his body. She was dressed in a multilayered black to gray ombre silk dress with layers that would float around her like a cloud when the time came. Her silver-blonde hair was swept up. She thought the whole tableau was fucking ridiculous, but everyone else loved it so she went along obediently. She warned herself sternly not to start thinking about shit that was going to make her get a case of the giggles.

The minutes slipped away. Her cotton-padded ears

pounded heavily. Someone shoved a mug of hot water with lemon into her hand, and she took a deep swallow. Then Macon was lifting her and murmuring into her ear to close her eyes and trust him, so she did. Her lungs constricted. As his steps carried him to the glowing mark on their small platform, she rested her head on his chest and breathed him in. He never quite shook the scent of cedar, woodsmoke, and the clean scent of the desert these days. No matter what collection of scents clung to him, he would always smell like home to her. She thought of that, and her breath came back.

When she finally opened her eyes, she was standing in the dark, and then the spotlight was sliding over them. She gazed into his eyes as the full orchestra transitioned between songs and faded until it was just strings. The nearly transparent silk panels began to blow around their feet, until they were floating at their full height and swirled like a cyclone around them. Small, white LED lights cut across the silk intermittently, like glowing streaks of rain. They were contained in a column of light, just as Matieu promised. Macon's fingers came to her chin, as was rehearsed. She lifted her hand to his bicep, as practiced. Her ring sparkled brightly in the stage lights.

They stood at the eye of a storm made of silk and light. The voices of the chorus and stringed instruments rose. Looking into his eyes, George didn't think of the audience for even a second. Her buzzing body knew what to do even when her brain stopped processing. Their voices wove together, and their performance of the heart-rending love song he made for her transcended any musical experience Georgia ever had. Which was significant, considering how George felt about making music – which was to say, she felt about it the same way other people seemed to feel about their gods.

It seemed to be over before she could blink, and Macon lifted her into his embrace and carried her back into the shadows. She felt dazed and hot all over with the buzzing anxiety that began when the performances started and progressively built into a steady, churning rumble through her muscles. Macon let her down when they reached backstage, and she swayed on her feet alarmingly. He picked her right back up again and stalked down the hall until he found a door out of the venue. He nodded curtly at the security guard, who pushed the door open for Macon and let him escape into the cold, winter night. He carried her through the organized chaos of generators and heat lamps, snaking power cords, pop-up tents, past the curious eyes of the event staff who'd come out for breaks and snacks and smokes during the performances. Finally, they reached the boulevard, and George squirmed in his arms.

He set her on her feet again and kept a bracing hand at her hip until he knew she was steady. He watched her carefully as she gulped deep breaths of the cold air until her skin stopped burning.

She exhaled in relief and looked up at him. "I can't believe we just did that," she said, her voice faint and full of wonder. "We got through it. I didn't even puke or pass out, or anything." Macon laughed softly. "Was it okay? I hardly remember it already. It feels like I dreamed it."

"You did so fucking good, baby." His eyes shone as he watched her. "You're so goddamned beautiful, Georgia. I'm so proud you're mine."

She ducked her head and smashed into him suddenly as she threw her arms around his middle and buried her face in his damp chest. "We have to go back in and get changed before the ceremony starts." She sighed.

"There's time, baby. We can stay out here as long as you need."

"I'll be nervous about it until we're back in our seats. Let's just get it over with."

He smiled and released her, then snagged her hand in his before they moved back through the backstage chaos and into the fray.

George squinted her eyes against the bright sunlight, disoriented for several long seconds until she remembered they spent the night in a hotel. Next to her Macon stirred, and she rolled over and threw her arms around him.

"Mmmphh," he said into the pillow.

George suddenly gasped and sat bolt upright in bed. She twisted to look around the room. On the couch she could see Macon's crumpled designer suit, and her silver gown sparkling on the floor. She could have sworn she dreamed the whole thing. "Babe, you won two fucking Grammys last night." She fell back into the pillows with an expression of disbelief.

Macon rolled over and pulled her into his arms without opening his eyes. He pushed his face into the space at the curve of her shoulder. "They'll make beautiful paperweights," his muffled voice came from her neck.

She laughed. "Come on, admit you care a little."

He rested his chin on her shoulder. "Of course I do. The proud part of me cares, but it's all kinda bullshit, you know? The prize was that I got to share that stage with you. That performance meant more to me than anything I've done in my career." He kissed her ear. "I was thinking about rolling around in these blankets with you all day, but I think we're supposed to meet Lucia and company for breakfast in an hour."

Georgia reached over to turn on her phone and cringed at the deluge of notifications. "Here we go again."

"Before you look at it, are we taking bets on engagement speculation?" Macon grinned. "You know that hand placement they wanted was to show off the ring."

George rolled her eyes.

"Hey, at least I got us out of the red-carpet bullshit," he reminded her. "They had to get something out of us for the gossip mill."

"I think they got plenty. You're forty-five and you just won your first two Grammys on the cusp of your retirement. That's a good story."

He shook his head and smiled slightly as his eyes ran over her. "It's not as good as a love story." He jerked his chin at the phone. "Let's see who's right. Loser gets absolutely *railed* in the shower before we leave."

She laughed and her eyes narrowed. "I'll take your bet, sir."

And even though she handily lost, it didn't really seem important by the time she finally arrived, wrung out and relaxed, to brunch. When they got there forty-five minutes late, both radiating glowing satisfaction and contentment, Lucia didn't even mention it.

Epilogue

Astravore

(n.) A soul that keeps feeding on hope even after disappointment; light-hungry, resilient, unbreakable.

George leaned back against Macon's chest as the hammock moved softly from side to side. She gazed out over the violet desert as the gold moon pulled free of the mountain peaks. "Cheers, we did it."

"It was cool to have them here, but sending them back was pretty great, too." Macon admitted. "Can you imagine what it would have been like to have both of them in LA? Alone?" He wiped his hand over his face wearily.

She made a noise of agreement. "I think it all worked out best for all of us." They were both tired after a month of juggling Michael and Jack, in addition to dealing with a busy studio schedule. When Macon decided to sell the tour bus, they'd come up with the idea of driving to Indy and picking up the kids and Barbara for its last voyage. Their three visitors left for the airport in the back of the studio assistant's minivan less than an hour ago, and both of them were grateful for the deep quiet.

"It was crazy today at the barn. I was worried I wasn't going to make it back in time to say goodbye." George yawned.

The studio had been booked solid for the past six months, and between producing for major artists and George's pro-bono side project recording demos for undiscovered artists, she was at full capacity.

"That new piece you did with Lazee Boi is gonna be huge. When are you releasing it?"

"I'm not sure," she answered. "The band's going on their first tour in six months, so I think they'll start dropping singles as soon as they get the masters back."

"Look at you, out there killing it." Macon squeezed her and kissed her hair. "Stella said the phone has been ringing off the hook for the past six weeks. We're gonna have to get our assistant an assistant."

"Well, the wedding bookings will cover more staff. That was such a smart idea, babe." She craned her neck to look up at him adoringly. He smiled softly and kissed the tip of her nose.

"Speaking of weddings…"

"Ugh." George looked out at the desert. "I don't even have time to think about it."

"It's next month, Mrs. Macon," he said with a stern look. "You'd better start thinking about it."

"You know I can't take your last name, right?"

"Why? How will everyone know you're my property?"

She laughed and smacked him indignantly. "Yeah, no. I'm not going to be Macon, Georgia."

"Fine. Maybe we pick a new last name for both of us."

"But then I can't call you 'Macon.'"

"Maybe I'll change my first name to Macon. There are no rules."

She laughed again. "I don't have it in me to argue with

you about this." She took a deep breath and exhaled. "I'm so wrecked after the boys. I can't believe I managed to keep it all together while they were here."

"They were pretty intense."

"That's kids for you. Maybe next time we try two weeks instead of a full month," she teased. "That was your idea, by the way. Just in case you forgot."

Macon sighed. "I know. Tonight, baby, I'm going to sleep like a rock. Tomorrow, I'm going to fuck you on the kitchen counter, just because I can."

She giggled. "I'm glad to have our space back, too."

"I have now learned just how long a month can be," Macon said with a chagrined expression. "It wasn't so bad until Jack started getting in bed with us in the middle of the night."

"Aw, I know. That sweet little baby."

"That sweet little baby inserted himself between me and my future wife every night for two weeks. I'm so glad we don't have kids. I'm not above being jealous of a child for how much of your attention they'd take. I'd fight a baby for you."

George burst out laughing. "One reason among many I'm glad we're both childless. I don't need you fighting babies."

Macon kissed the back of her ear and she shivered.

"How tired are you, exactly?" George asked breathlessly.

"I've probably got enough energy to get you downstairs, undressed, and properly satisfied before I'm comatose."

"Why wait?" George said softly with a mischievous little smile. "There's no one around for miles. Isn't that why we bought the place?"

"Mm," Macon hummed. He paused to close his teeth

around her ear. "That's a good point. That's exactly why we bought the place." He reached around and began to unfasten her shirt buttons.

The stars came out as they wrapped their limbs together. Macon played her body like a fine and rare instrument — carefully, skillfully, masterfully coaxing from it the dulcet sighs building to her crescendo. The subtle music of the night began and the sweet sounds of the pleasure they took in each other blew away softly across the desert, accompanied by the whispering rush of the wind in the pines, the distant howl of a coyote, and the soft rhythmic calls of an owl. She arched in his arms as a warm wind blew over them, and her heart beat in double-time as she watched his face transform in ecstasy for her.

It was more of a happy ending than she ever thought she'd have, maybe more than she deserved. After searching for her place in the world for so long, it turned out the only home she ever needed was right here in the circle of his embrace.

A NOTE TO MY READERS

This story was intensely personal. I began it in 2022, but stopped writing when I realized I couldn't publish if any of the real characters were still living. Then, our power went out for a week and I decided to write it this autumn, after the deaths of both my grandparents this year. And here we are with our handful of little silver linings.

If you liked it, please leave a review for me where you purchased it – this is crucial to getting it in front of new readers! I'm currently working on the audiobook version of this, so stay tuned for that addition in 2026.

Several of my pre-readers asked about the words I chose for the chapter headings, so I'd like to give a little insight. About half of them are from *The Dictionary of Obscure Sorrows*, by John Koenig – one of my favorite books. The other words are mostly borrowed from other languages and describe emotional states we don't have words for in English. It was such a satisfying several weeks of research, to be buried in such linguistic treasures, while I worked out which to include.

Thank you again for reading. I hope you enjoyed it!

See you 'round, cutie.
xxx Adlynn

Sign up for my mailing list
at AdlynnAster.com

www.ingramcontent.com/pod-product-compliance
Lightning Source LLC
Chambersburg PA
CBHW030758200726

PP18592100001B/6